WAYAH
of the
Real People

WAYAH
of the
Real People

WILLIAM O. STEELE

ILLUSTRATED BY ISA BARNETT

WILLIAMSBURG, VIRGINIA

COLONIAL WILLIAMSBURG

Distributed by

HOLT, RINEHART AND WINSTON, INC.

New York

To all members of the Chattanooga Public Library Staff who serve me and keep me cheered—and especially to those three "Glorious Leaders" whose efforts have often extended beyond the outer limits of duty:

Kathryn Arnold
Eloise Fisher
Hanna Sayers

Foreword

The story of Wayah of the Real People takes place during the years 1752 and 1753. It is fiction. It tells of one year in the life of a Cherokee boy from Chota who left his wilderness home to go to Brafferton Hall, the school for Indian boys at the College of William and Mary in Williamsburg, Virginia. He hoped that this would help his town gain the leadership of the Cherokee nation. At that time the Cherokees, the Real People, lived in the southern Appalachians, and the tribe was split into four separate parts. Rivalry and dissension among these factions became intense in the 1750's as each struggled to control the whole tribe. Chota, Wayah's town, and Great Tellico were the main rivals for power.

Brafferton Hall still stands on the old campus of the College of William and Mary. The impressive, three-story brick building has suffered little damage over the years since it was built by the estate of Robert Boyle, British scientist and inventor of the air pump. Boyle wanted his wealth used after his death for the advancement of the Christian religion among the heathen. A large part of his estate was invested in the manor of Brafferton in Yorkshire, England. From the yearly rents of this investment came the money to build Brafferton Hall at the College and to support the Indians who enrolled there.

Brafferton's graduates, it was hoped, would go forth and persuade other Indians to adopt the Christian faith. Through religion and education, in time the many Indian nations would come to understand the white man's way of life and choose it as their own. Then, Indian wars and massacres that had plagued the Virginia colonists through the early days of settlement would no longer take place, and the colony's expansion inland from the Atlantic coastal strip could proceed peacefully.

These hopeful plans did not succeed. Up to the time of the Revolutionary War, when the support of the Boyle Charity ceased, no Indian boy had stayed at Brafferton long enough to become a minister. And, so far as is known, none ever returned to his tribe to teach or preach. Rather, it appears that the Brafferton students resumed their ways of tribal life, resenting the white intruders upon their lands and resisting them as much as ever.

While many of the College records have been lost and information on the Indian students is difficult to find, it is known that Cherokee boys like Wayah attended Brafferton Hall. Governor Dinwiddie wrote Chota's headman in 1756 and begged that the next boys sent to the school be only about eight years in age. The older Cherokee boys who had come to Brafferton found their confinement too irksome and had run away. History also tells that Chota eventually outmaneuvered Great Tellico to become the capital of the Cherokee Nation.

Contents

1. The Long Person   1
2. The Breechclout Student   8
3. Brafferton Hall   15
4. Wolf Puts on a New Skin   23
5. The Winking Magic Stone   33
6. Trouble   42
7. "In the Gales"   52
8. Worries and a Sign   64
9. The Wrong Kind of Cherokee   74
10. At the Theatre   83
11. Fever Dreams   92
12. "Adam Wolf Done It!"   102
13. Two Sticks Returns   111
14. Chota   119

WAYAH
of the
Real People

- 1 -

The Long Person

A GREAT pool of darkness lay over the land of the Cherokees. Beside the Little Tennessee River the town of Chota slept out the last of the June night. In one hut Wayah, the Wolf, opened his eyes. Through the smoke hole in the roof he saw two bright stars fade slowly from the sky. A ball of fear rolled around inside him. This was the day.

He sat up on his cane bed. His mother and his father and his younger brother were still sleeping on the couches ranged along the sides of the dwelling. Slipping across the earth floor he raised the skin flap across the doorway. Soon it would be light. His grandfather would be waiting.

Dressed only in his breechclout he stepped out into the fresh morning air. No one stirred in the dusty streets. Even the dogs only raised an ear as he passed. He gave a little shiver, not of cold, but excitement. It was the day of his departure.

The birds began to call uncertainly. Now to the east the sky lightened and he could plainly see the mountains, a dark purple rim to this land of the Cherokees, the Real People.

Beyond those high peaks in the land of the white skins the sun was rising also. There, too, the birds were calling and a little wind was boiling in the tops of poplar tree and beech. But what other strange things were going on there? He had heard such queer tales, from traders and from grown people, about the houses of the whites, and the strange craft pulled by horses and the mysterious things white men did and wore and ate.

Now he was going to see it all for himself. He, Wayah, the Wolf, was going among the white men to learn exactly what they did and didn't do.

Under his breastbone there was the feeling he had when he stood on the cliff's high edges and made ready to jump down, down, down into the foam-specked river. Swooping through the air, rushing toward the water was exciting, but it was a little fearful too. It frightened him now to think what the white men might do to him, one lone eleven-year-old boy, when he reached their land.

A horse, trailing a broken rope, trotted by at the end of the street. Wayah gave a start. It would soon be dawn. What was he doing standing here? He must find his grandfather before sunrise.

There, at the river's edge, he spied the tall thin figure. He ran, though he knew Otonee wouldn't like it. This was an important occasion and it should be approached slowly and with gravity.

"Si-yu, Grandfather," Wayah gasped.

"And greetings to you, my son," replied Otonee.

He said nothing more and Wayah too was silent. They both turned and faced the Long Human Person, the ever-running river whose many tongues spoke constantly and quietly, and who never said anything but words of wisdom. It seemed to Wayah that his grandfather's voice was like the voice of the river, wise and calm and beautiful, as he began his prayer. The old man praised the river for its beauty and gentleness and strength. He asked its help on the boy's long journey and the many tasks which awaited him.

Out of the corner of his eye Wayah watched his grandfather. Oh, how he loved him. Though this man was Wayah's father's father, and not, therefore, an important member of his family,

Wayah had always loved him best. Once he had been a mighty warrior and a skillful game hunter. Even now he was a respected member of the town elders.

Otonee was always patient, always kind, always willing to listen to a small boy's troubles, to tell him a marvelous tale of the Real People, to help his unskilled hands fashion a flint arrowhead or a fishhook of bone. Why practically everything Wayah knew his grandfather had taught him, how to sing the bear from its den, where the deer feed on warm fall days, how to find his way through the forest no matter how far he wandered, how to have good luck in hunting, how to avoid water cannibals and other evil spirits.

Many of the Cherokees no longer thought it was necessary to know these things. These customs were old and useless and best forgotten. Some would have thought Otonee and Wayah foolish for coming here to ask help of the river for Wayah's venture. Sometimes, secretly, Wayah himself thought the old ways were a little silly. But he loved and trusted his grandfather. He would do as Otonee asked.

Now the prayer was finished and Otonee said, "The Day Dweller comes. Go to water."

Wayah stepped into the river. He did not feel foolish at all. The water's cool hands seemed to hold him kindly, and as he dipped seven times under the surface, he knew that the river blessed him with its strength and its cleanliness. As he rose the last time, a long red finger of sunlight reached across the river and touched him. His life belonged to the Long Person now.

As the boy emerged, Otonee stood rubbing his right arm. "Does it pain you, Grandfather?" asked the Wolf.

The old man sighed. "Yes. It is because my daughter will cook my food in the white man's brass pot," he answered. "I have asked and asked her to make stew in a clay pot. And she does for a while, for she is a good daughter. Then the pot cracks and she starts using the brass one again. Arg! The pain comes back."

He rubbed his arm again, his wrinkled fingers digging into the muscles. Though he had been often to the medicine man, the intruder still remained in his arm.

-4-

Wayah stared at Otonee. Was this true? He himself often ate food cooked in brass pots. Yet his arm had never ached except that time he fell from a tree on it. Now that he was going to live among the whites, he would be continually eating from their pots and bowls. He frowned, uneasy and apprehensive.

Otonee, looking down at him, laughed. "Do not worry, little Wolf," he reassured the boy. "Evil spirits always seek out the old and the weak to hurt."

Wayah nodded, relieved. It was going to be hard enough living among the Virginians without having aches and pains to add to his troubles. There would be much for him to do. He must learn about the little black talking marks that the white man put on paper and thought so highly of. He must learn of their strange gods too, and whatever else they had locked away in the school.

It *was* going to be hard. Yet, in a way he could hardly wait to leave. He was anxious to see new and strange sights. He wanted to see the soldiers of the English king with their red coats and gold buttons, to see the great boats with guns big as an Indian dugout.

Together they climbed the riverbank toward the town.

"Perhaps some day the white men will go away and leave us in peace," Otonee spoke. "Perhaps then the Real People will use clay pots once more and hunt with bows and arrows again. Perhaps we will be a strong people as we once were before the whites came."

Perhaps so, thought Wayah. The white men were evil. He knew this for Otonee had told him, and not just Otonee. Many of the Real People hated the whites. They hated them not only because they came with guns and killing, but because they made the young men discontented and lazy and drunken, because now many people no longer believed in the old ways, in the sacredness of sky and earth and water. Every time a brave killed a deer without saying the hunting prayers, the old men watched with troubled eyes. No wonder game was getting scarce!

And yet, Wayah knew how useful it was to have a brass pot that did not crack, and a gun bought from the traders which was so much finer to use than silent old-fashioned bows and arrows. Making a bow and arrows was hard work and took a long time.

"I am only your father's father," went on Otonee. "It is not for me to say what you should do. It is for your mother and her people to decide. But I hope you will not forget the things I have taught you, Wayah. Remember the paths we have walked, the same paths that our fathers walked, and their fathers. Do not turn aside from them."

Wayah threw up his head proudly. The Real People had a long and noble history. His tribe had survived much hardship. He would never forget. He would always remember.

They reached the open square. Children yelled and chased each other, dogs barking at their heels. A little heron flew slowly overhead. A war party filed by and got in the dugouts tied below. They were going against the French on the great river far to the west. The braves each carried a rifle.

Otonee paid the warriors no heed. He went right on talking. "An Indian who takes on the white man's ways is like an oak tree struck by lightning," warned Otonee. "As lightning splits the oak's trunk in two, so the white man's touch splits the red man. He is no longer one good tree, but two worthless ones, part white, part Indian, no good to either tribe."

Now Wayah was truly troubled. Who would want such a thing to happen? That was certainly not what his mother's father had told him. This other grandfather had said, "You will be a chain binding the white man to the Cherokee in ties of friendship. Now the Virginians will know that we wish to live in peace with them, for we have sent them our son to live among them and learn from them. Now, you, Wayah, the Wolf, will help your people by doing this."

His mother's brothers had urged him to go. Wayah understood the white man's talk though his tongue was too thick to shape the words. His mother had nursed a sick trader in their hot house last winter and the white man had taught him much. Of all the children in Chota he was the best able to go.

His uncles knew this. "The Great Man in Carolina has cut off our supply of lead and powder, of knives and blankets and pots," they had said. "Our people mourn for goods. Without these things Chota will die. The Virginians have promised to send these things

to us and to trade with us if you go to their school and spend a year among them. Do not refuse. Help your people by going."

Now Wayah put his hands to his head in confusion. He felt jerked first one way, then the other. The queer feeling under his breastbone changed to a sharp pain.

He stared around at the tall trees and the wide river and the far-off hills, the color of sadness. Oh, how could he go away and leave Chota and his family and friends? How could he leave when leaving would make him a horrible, useless thing, not fit to be a warrior of the Real People?

"Grandfather," he whispered. "I cannot go. Let me stay."

Otonee's voice was mourning. "I cannot keep you here. Only your mother's people have that power. But remember what I have told you. Hold fast and true to Indian ways."

He grabbed the Wolf with his old hands and brought his face close to the boy's. "And remember also, a Cherokee boy meets his fate bravely. Whatever happens to him, even death from the Night Land, he never flinches or cries out."

Otonee turned and walked away. Wayah watched him go. It was true. He had no choice. He had to go and live among the Virginians. He had to go no matter what, even if it meant that he would become as ugly and useless as a tree split by lightning.

- 2 -

The Breechclout Student

WAYAH jogged along the trail behind his uncle, Two Sticks. Since leaving Chota ten days before, they had kept to this same fast pace. Wayah would have liked to go more slowly, but a Cherokee boy did not ask for special consideration. He did what his uncle told him. If he was tired, he gritted his teeth and pressed on just the same. What a man could do, Wayah was determined to do also.

Besides, he told himself, it was best this way. He had no room in his head or his chest for anything but running. He had no place for thoughts of what lay ahead of him, or for worry or fear. Instead the steady thump of his own feet and the sight of his uncle's strong brown legs going up and down filled his whole world. The handle of his tomahawk slapped against his thigh and his pack bounced gently on his back. Thump, slap, bounce, thump, slap, bounce, the rhythm went on and on endlessly, so that Wayah ran without thinking, without feeling.

Two Sticks had kept them to a steady gait all the way. Their only halts had been to sleep at night, though once Wayah ripped his moccasin and they stopped while he patched it. There had been much to see on the journey. Especially Wayah had desired to pause and ask his uncle about the great pile of stones in a mountain pass. The heap commemorated some long-ago event, some great battle or disaster. Wayah would have liked to hear about it from his uncle. No, Two Sticks rushed past the place without even glancing at it.

There had been many other things in the great forests for a boy to investigate if he had the time. But the Wolf and Two Sticks had set out on a journey. To reach the end of the journey was what mattered. The boy knew that was what his uncle had his mind set on. Two Sticks would never consider stopping. This was not like hunting or going visiting. This was like going to war. There was a place to get to and they would get there as quickly as possible.

Wayah had kept on hoping, however, that Two Sticks would do just a little hunting. Rabbits had flashed across the trail often, turkeys had scattered through the bushes, deer had splashed away up the streams from fording places. How good one of these would have tasted, fresh-killed and roasted. Two Sticks had seemed not to notice, no matter how close the game came. The Wolf had tried not to sigh as he chewed on his dried meat and corn at every meal.

Now as they loped along, Wayah noticed a difference from their other days of travel. Two Sticks had lost the rhythm of his pace. He hesitated often and once he even stumbled.

Wayah knew what the matter was. He did not even need his uncle's remark, thrown over his shoulder, "Not far now." It didn't take keen eyes to see that the woods had a different look here. Some of the stillness and secrecy was gone. There was no game anywhere that the Wolf could see. This was white man's country; the whites lived here as thick as snakes in a den and Two Sticks was uneasy.

They passed many places where the trees had been cut and cleared. Another trail joined the one they were using and now fields stood out on either side of this two track roadway. Many were fenced. Wayah thought it was foolish to put a fence around a field of corn, as though the stalks could walk away.

More and more travelers filled the road, more than the two

Cherokees had met all the other days put together. Two Sticks seemed suspicious of all as they approached or passed. He clutched his rifle tighter, he tilted his head to catch any movement. Yet, nothing happened. No one stopped them, and Two Sticks led on. Behind him Wayah lagged and panted, conscious of his aching chest, his weary legs, not sure that he could keep up much longer.

They came to a dwelling, a big log house. Wayah stared back over his shoulder. Was that the kind of place he was going to have to live in? What a curious way to build a hut! It must take many men to lift those logs, he thought. The Cherokees used fewer logs, placed them upright in the ground, and had a much better house with less work.

There were no other houses of the white skins to see. Occasionally through the trees he glimpsed odd shapes and strange angles like nothing he had ever seen before. He guessed these must be houses and that perhaps the whites did not like to live on the trails as Indians did.

The June sun beat down and on the road behind them the dust they had stirred up settled down in little dying swirls. The Wolf was thirsty. His dry tongue felt stiff in his mouth. He hoped they were going to stop soon.

It was almost midday before Two Sticks turned aside and struck off into the woods, leaving the sunny trail. Wayah was glad of the cool shade. A few minutes later they came to a spring. The warrior threw off his pack and drank. Wayah waited politely till he was through. Then he too buried his face in the cold clear water and drank.

It must be a favorite stopping place, the boy thought, as he sat up and looked around. There were scattered ashes and half-burnt sticks all about. Likely his uncle had been here before. Two Sticks was a great warrior and an important man in the tribe. In time he would be a chief. He had been to Williamsburg before.

Now his uncle handed him a strip of dried meat. The Wolf began to chew it. Where would his next meal be coming from? After his uncle left, there would be no one to provide meat for him. He himself had no weapon except his tomahawk—no knife, no gun, no bow. Game was scarce hereabouts. Two Sticks could talk all he wished about food being provided for him at the school. With no family or friends to hunt for him who was going to fill his cooking pot with meat?

He lay on his back staring up, remembering Chota. The sky was the same at home and the trees and the earth. Only he, Wayah, the Wolf, was different, waiting here with a tight knot in his chest while Cherokee boys were running and laughing in the fields by the river, while his father was setting a fish trap and his mother was baking bread of dried persimmon meal. He felt very mournful and sat up suddenly.

Two Sticks was standing across the spring. The sight of him made the Wolf almost cry aloud with pleasure. His uncle was wearing breeches, bright blue ones with silver buckles at the knee. He had on a red and white striped ruffled shirt, white stockings covered his great muscled legs, little brass bells dangled from the ties of his moccasins, and he had twisted a green and gold ribbon into his scalplock.

It seemed to the boy that he had never seen anything so beautiful. He knew Two Sticks had paid many deerskins to the trader for this finery. But oh, it had been worth it! Who could deny that here was a great man, a hero among heroes?

"Uncle, my eyes are dazzled," he said softly.

Two Sticks smiled. He took a mirror and admired himself, angling the glass first one way, then another. At last he set it up on a low limb. Staring into it, he dipped a finger into a little bag of vermillion paint and drew two wavy lines across his forehead. His cheeks were already tattooed in a pattern of black.

Now Two Sticks walked back and forth as though to show off his elegance to the crawfish in the spring or the clumps of grass around it. He walked rather stiffly and the boy could see that he was not really comfortable in such tight fitting clothes.

"These are good talking clothes," the warrior said. "I could never fight in them." He pulled at the shirt where it bound across the shoulders and cut into his neck. He was sweating greatly.

Watching him, Wayah felt suddenly very free and cool and easy in his flap and moccasins. "Otonee is right," he thought. "An Indian should not wear white men's clothes."

Did these clothes make Two Sticks a white man? Did they change his copper skin and tattooed cheeks or take away his scalp-lock? No. Still, even Grandfather would have to admit that Two Sticks' clothes were beautiful and that never in old tribal days had any one worn such handsome dress.

The Wolf sighed. It was puzzling. His hand rested on his tomahawk, a fine new one with a steel head, easily bought from the trader. No one could deny that such axes were better than the stone ones, made by hand, which grew dull in a few blows and needed much effort to sharpen.

The white man's axe was better and his gun was better than a bow and arrow. These things the Cherokees needed and must have from the white men. Now he, Wayah, was going to school in Virginia so that the Virginians would trade with the Real People and bring them these good things. Much depended on him, on one lone Cherokee boy who spoke only a few words of English and who had never traveled more than the next valley away from Chota before in his whole life.

"Are you not wearing the shirt you brought in your bundle?" Two Sticks asked, as he gathered up his belongings. "The one I bought for you from the trader?"

Wayah did not want to hurt his uncle's feelings. The shirt had been a gift to show that his mother's brother was proud of him and wanted him to appear at the school at least partly dressed in the white man's clothes. But Wayah was reluctant. The shirt looked uncomfortable. Soon enough he would be wearing the white man's clothes. Soon enough he would forget the feel of wind and sun on his bare back.

For this last little while he would be an Indian. He would go to the school as only himself, Wayah, one of the Real People. Let them do as they liked with him after that.

"You say I will get clothes?" the boy asked.

Two Sticks glanced up. "Clothes. Food. A place to sleep. These were promised."

"Then, Uncle, if you do not mind, I won't wear the shirt," the Wolf said. "Take it to my brother. He is young. He has never owned a fine shirt. It would please him."

The warrior nodded. "It is good," he agreed. "Your heart speaks kind thoughts. It will be so."

The Wolf dusted his breechclout. He rearranged the quill of cane which held his hair in one strand at the back. Tightening his belt, he then straightened the tomahawk in the sling at his side. As simply and quickly as that he was ready.

Two Sticks hid their bundles and his rifle in a hollow tree. "Now it is time to go," he said to the boy.

Wayah's heart bumped inside the branches of his ribs. What lay ahead of him in this foreign land, among these strange people? Would anyone care what happened to him through the endless days stretching ahead? His shoulders sagged. He was lost, as good as dead.

Then, suddenly, he heard his grandfather's voice cry out, "Shame, shame, shame!"

He raised his head and a crow was cawing at him from the tree tops. But the sign was powerful and it came at a good time. It reminded him what he must do and who he was.

Whatever happened, he had to bear it bravely for his people. He was a Cherokee. That was his courage. He drew a deep breath into his lungs and said, "I am ready, Uncle."

The tiny bells on Two Sticks moccasins jingled. Wayah fell in behind him and they set out through the woods.

- 3 -

Brafferton Hall

BEFORE the Indians among the trees were three houses of giant size, with many openings. Some of the openings had a covering which flashed, like the face of a still pool, when the sun struck it. These houses were built of a curious small red stone like nothing Wayah had ever seen before. He wondered where the white men found so many of these stones, all straight-sided and alike.

Where would he live? He hoped it would be in the large house which had another house, hardly as big as a Cherokee hot house, sitting up on top of it, like a scalplock. That would be a wonderful place to live. But no, that must surely be the dwelling place for the great chief of all Virginia. It was so fine a building.

He turned to ask his uncle, only to find Two Sticks hurrying along a path that ran between rows of bushes and trees. Wayah ran after him. Why were the trees left growing here? In Chota, in the town, there were only a few mulberry and pawpaw trees, not elms and maples and oaks. Lightning struck such big trees, winds blew them over, catamounts and even human enemies hid in their branches. They were dangerous so close to the huts. Besides, the forest was full of trees, why let them grow in a town?

The sound of boys' voices came nearer as the Indians approached the house on the left. Two Sticks glanced up when they stopped before it. "I have gazed out that opening high up there," he pointed proudly. "You will live there."

Wayah did not even look. His eyes were on the cleared yard to one side where many white boys ran and shouted. Near him two boys pitched a round flat disc at a hole in the ground. Beyond them was a boy with a cloth tied over his eyes. His hair was the color of copper, a thing that made Wayah's heart bump with surprise. Some other boys dashed up and hit the redheaded one and then dodged away from his groping hands.

This must be a kind of punishment, the Wolf thought. What queer ways the white people had. But there, now, that was a game, he felt sure, and it was a good one too. Two small boys rode on the shoulders of bigger boys, like horses. The small boys pulled and wrestled and tugged at one another.

Wayah couldn't help grinning as he watched, and when one boy finally unhorsed the other, he could hardly suppress a shout. Not that he would have been heard. The losers were protesting wildly.

Suddenly one of the boys caught sight of the two Indians. He pointed and yelled, and quiet fell over the playground. The whites stared boldly and Wayah dropped his eyes. He longed to get behind Two Sticks and hide, but he would not. He was a Cherokee boy. He was proud, he was brave. Let them look till the ravens pecked their eyes out.

But his innards had turned to water. He must spend a long year with these people with their cruel and ugly pale faces and their strange clothes and their alien ways. It would be a long year surely. He could feel the way the days would drag by and how each one would cut and lacerate his flesh—a prisoner tied to the stake to be tortured for a year.

"Oh, Uncle," he cried out suddenly. "Don't forget me. Come for me as soon as the time is up!"

His mother's oldest brother frowned. Wayah cringed. Had he

made Two Sticks angry? His uncle was a warrior, a great man. If he was not afraid, it was because he had no reason to be. But he, the Wolf, was only a boy. In a year, the whole tribe might have forgotten him. They might be busy hunting or at war, and no one would think of Wayah away off living as one of the white people.

"How could I forget?" asked Two Sticks almost crossly. "You have come here to make sure my warriors and I get guns and powder and the Real People the goods they desire. We need you and we will not forget."

He smiled a little. "Besides, Otonee will not let me forget. Never! Before the corn tassels next summer I will return for you."

Wayah straightened his shoulders. Otonee would never forget. And was he not under the protection of the Long Person? There was nothing for him to fear. He should have remembered. It was womanish to be frightened. He looked boldly back at the white boys. He was not afraid. But where were the Indians who went to this school?

One of the boys ran toward the door. "Master Dawson, Master Dawson!" he shouted.

Several more boys ran out of the building to see what was causing the disturbance. After a few minutes a white man appeared in the door. At the sight of him, Wayah drew back in alarm. He was wearing a long black robe that fell almost to his feet. His face and hands were as white as snow.

Why were the white people in Williamsburg so very white? Wayah wondered. The traders and scouts who came to Chota were paler than Indians, but they still were tanned and brown, their cheeks and lips had color in them. This man was like a man who had lived all his life in a cave, his skin was the color of death, even his hair was pale, and his eyes—Wayah turned his own eyes away. He could not bear to look at those blind staring blue things.

The schoolmaster came forward and took Two Sticks by the hand. "I am the Reverend Thomas Dawson," he said, and his voice was as light and dry as grasses brushing against each other. But it was a kind voice. Wayah couldn't help liking it. "What is your name?"

"He wants to know your name, Uncle," Wayah whispered.

Two Sticks answered. He gave Wayah a little shove forward. "Boy for school," he said gruffly. He had spent many hours learning these English words.

The master bent and put his hand under the boy's chin. Wayah set his jaw and tried not to flinch. But the white man's hand was firm and warm and friendly. He raised Wayah's head and Wayah tried not to look at the dreadful bleached eyes.

"And what is your name?" asked Thomas Dawson.

"I am Wolf," answered Wayah calmly. He was surprised to hear himself. Usually his English words came out slowly and in a mutter.

Master Dawson laughed. "And a fine young cub you are too," he said. "Welcome to Brafferton Hall, young Wolf. We are right glad to have you. We have much to teach a lad such as you. And especially we want to teach you of our God and his undying love and the eternal life He promises you."

Two Sticks, standing with arms folded and his face as still as a stone, gave Wayah a sharp kick.

"He speaks too fast," said Wayah to his uncle. "I can not understand." He shook his head at Master Dawson, who seemed to know what he meant.

"Welcome to Brafferton Hall," he repeated slowly. "We will teach you many great things."

Wayah nodded. He understood "welcome" and "teach" anyway. But Two Sticks was impatient. He, after all, was the warrior and head man. He did not like having to wait. "Din-wid, Din-wid," he growled.

Master Dawson looked puzzled. "Are you Shawnees?" he asked. "We have a Shawnee boy with us." He turned and shouted a name.

In a minute an Indian boy came out of the house. He was big and tall and broad shouldered. His face was still, too, like Two Sticks', but it was a different stillness. It was like the stillness of the coiled rattlesnake, waiting, waiting. In the back of his black eyes burned a little flame of hunger and hatred. Wayah had seen such a thing before, in the eyes of a fox someone had kept tied in the village.

He had been afraid he would be the only Indian boy in the

school. Now he knew he wasn't. But would it not be worse to be here with a Shawnee boy, a member of a Nation with whom the Cherokees had fought since time out of mind, and a Shawnee boy whose very skin was drawn tight with hate?

"This is our Shawnee boy, William Squirrel," said Dawson. "Here are newcomers, William, and I do not think they understand me too well. Can you tell what tribe they are from?"

The Shawnee boy looked at them insolently. "Cherokee!" He almost spat the word.

The master's face lit up. "We have never before had a Cherokee boy," he cried. "Oh, this is splendid."

"Din-wid," grunted Two Sticks again.

Wayah glanced at him. He knew what Two Sticks wanted him to do. But, when his uncle left, Wayah would be parting with his family, his last contact with his home for a year, forever—who could tell? He would like to put that moment off as long as he could. But he knew it was useless. He might as well do what his uncle wished.

"Two Sticks speak with Chief Din-wid," the Wolf said haltingly. Out of the corner of his eye he watched fiercely to see who would laugh at his speech.

"Of course, of course," Master Dawson cried. He snatched the warrior by the hand and shook it vigorously. "We will treat the boy well. He will learn much," he said slowly and carefully.

Two Sticks nodded as if he understood.

"My brother is a good friend to Governor Dinwiddie," Master Dawson went on. "He is president of this college and lives right across the garden there. He will take you to the Governor's house in the town."

He turned to the Shawnee, "William, you and the other boys, take care of our new student. I'll only be a minute."

To Two Sticks he motioned and said, "Come." He trotted off along a path through the row of bushes toward the house opposite Brafferton, and the red man followed.

"Farewell, Uncle," Wayah called in Cherokee.

But Two Sticks only jerked his head. Now he was a head man in all his fine clothes, going to see the governor. It was not fit that

he should waste time with boys. Wayah knew this, but he watched, hoping his uncle would turn and look back one last time. Reluctantly he then faced the boys.

William Squirrel wheeled abruptly to go back into the school. Wayah gasped. On the left side the Shawnee boy had no hand! Only the stump of an arm swung by his hip. No wonder he was full of misery. Who could shoot a bow or even a rifle with only one hand? The Wolf wondered how such a terrible thing had happened.

Now the white boys came crowding up close. Wayah wished the teacher had not gone. He stood alone in a circle of white faces and though one or two grinned at him, it seemed to Wayah it was in no friendly fashion.

"What's your name?" asked one.

Wayah said nothing.

"What is your name?" repeated the boy, very loudly and slowly.

"Chief Sour Mush Face," answered another boy and the rest giggled. "Chief Pig Grunt," said another.

The biggest boy walked up to Wayah and pulled at his breechclout. "That's the smallest chance of clothes I ever saw. Reckon his name's Chief Pinch Penny, for he's too mean to buy breeches."

He gave Wayah a shove. The Wolf said nothing. He watched the big boy warily. "Or maybe Chief Starving Bear, for he's too poor to get decent food. His ribs stick out so far you could play a fine tune on them." He punched Wayah sharply in the ribs with his fingers.

"Leave him be, Grigley," said the redheaded boy suddenly. "He's not done anything to you."

"Or maybe we'll call him Chief John the Baptist," the big boy went on, "and serve up his head on a platter. Yes, I think that would be best."

He grabbed Wayah by his long hair and twisted his head to one side. "Right there, see? We'll cut it off right about there." He slashed his fingernail along Wayah's neck making a long scratch.

Wayah tried not to flinch.

The redheaded boy spoke again. "Oh, Grigley, you are a bully. You never pick on anybody who can fight you back."

Grigley ignored him. "John, run fetch Master's ferule."

"Fetch it yourself," said John with some spirit. He was a tiny boy with almost white hair.

Grigley reached out and seized him by an ear and began to twist it. "Fetch Master's ferule," he roared.

"All right, all right," gasped John. "Let me go." The bigger boy released him and John ran off rubbing his ear. In a minute he came back with a narrow paddle of wood with a hole in the center.

"Now," said Grigley, "we'll teach you a thing about white men you didn't know before. Hold out your hand." He raised the board and made a lunge for Wayah's hand. Swiftly the Cherokee boy knocked the ferule aside and sent it spinning into the dust.

Grigley's face turned red. He rushed for the paddle. As his fingers closed around the handle, Wayah slipped his tomahawk from its leather sling. He raised the weapon to throw.

"Look out, Grigley," screamed a boy. "He's going to kill you!"

- 4 -

Wolf Puts on a New Skin

THE tomahawk left Wayah's fingers with a sighing sound and the sunlight caught the blade as it spun over once. The boys gasped. The hatchet slammed into the ferule and cut it neatly in two. Grigley, white as a sheet, dropped the stump of the ferule from his hand.

Wayah could hardly hide his grin. It had been a good throw.

Grigley stared at the Indian boy with wide eyes. "You tried to kill me!" he shrieked suddenly. "You tried to kill me."

Wayah did not know what he meant. He drew himself up and stared sullenly around at the others. They were all talking and shouting at once, pressing close, waving their arms and fists.

"Fight, fight!"

"Hit him, Grigley!"

"Kill Grigley, Injun!"

The loud thick voices all around made Wayah dizzy. His breath came harshly and his heart quickened.

Grigley came forward. Wayah realized that he and this white boy were going to have a fight. His lip curled with disdain. The

white boy was bigger and heavier, but he was also clumsy and stiff. He would be no match for the Wolf's wiry muscles. Wayah began to enjoy himself. It would be a great pleasure to show these white skins what real strength and endurance were.

Grigley lunged at him and Wayah stepped aside and whacked him on the side of the head with his palm. The boys whooped louder than ever. Suddenly Master Dawson swept into their midst and seized Grigley by the shoulder and shook him hard.

"Grigley! What is this?" he cried.

Grigley staggered and then recovered himself. "Master," he said smoothly, "the Injun boy needs to be taught a lesson. He has split your ferule with his ax." He pointed to the pieces on the ground.

Master Dawson looked. "And who took my ferule from its place?" he asked sternly.

"John Pearson fetched it," Grigley answered.

There was a murmur among the boys. The redheaded boy muttered, "Oh, Grigley, you snake!"

Dawson looked around at his charges. "Is Grigley telling the truth?" he asked sharply. "Did Pearson fetch the ferule? Did the Indian cut it?"

The boys glanced at each other. Finally Pearson spoke. "I fetched it," he said in a low voice. "The Injun split it when Grigley tried to hit him with it."

"I was only trying to pick it up and take it back to the classroom," said Grigley hastily. "Maybe the Injun didn't understand. I'm sorry, sir."

Master Dawson looked from Grigley to Wayah. His eyes were a little sad. "Pearson, go inside," he said finally. "Wolf, you must give me your tomahawk." He spoke slowly and Wayah understood. "Here we do not carry weapons. Here we try to live by God's rule of forgiveness."

Wayah knew that it was true. None of the boys carried gun or knife, bow or tomahawk. "If an enemy came suddenly among us, we would all die," he thought. But he picked up the tomahawk and handed it to the master.

"It will be yours again, when school is done," Dawson promised. "In the meanwhile you will not need it."

He turned. "Grigley," he said, "it is a strange thing to me that you are so often the innocent victim of these excitements. There must be some reason why. Though you are never guilty of any wrongdoing, all these disturbances seem to hover about you. I hope you will examine your conscience thoroughly on this matter to see where the fault lies."

Grigley looked smug. The master hurried away into the school.

Wayah stood forlornly. He felt naked without his tomahawk among the pale, unfriendly faces. He had disgraced his people and already been in trouble. He had not understood what was said but he knew that the master had not been pleased with him. He hoped he had not lost his friendship. That would be bad. But it was comforting to know he had made an enemy of Grigley. An enemy he could understand. There would never be peace between him and that white boy. Their paths were plainly marked in red. About the others he did not know and the uncertainty scraped along his skin like a gar-tooth comb.

The Shawnee boy appeared from nowhere with three other Indians. They stood and stared at the Wolf while the white boys went back to their games and shouting.

Suddenly there was a terrible noise. Clang! Clang! Clang!

Wayah clutched his ears and cowered. He would have run, but the sound seemed to come from every direction. He did not know where to go to find safety. The white boys all began to flee toward the school, crowding in at the door. They must know. He would go there too, to take refuge from the blood-chilling voice—Clang! Whang! Clang! echoing and re-echoing.

Someone seized him by the arm. It was William Squirrel. His eyes squinted up with a contemptuous grin. "It is only the bell, frightened one," he said in English.

Wayah understood. He saw now that the white boys were unafraid. Though they were going into the school, the shoving and jostling was in fun. The redheaded boy turned to watch as the Indians walked toward the door.

But William Squirrel was a liar. Wayah knew. He had seen bells, tiny bells to tie on moccasins, fist-sized bells to hang around the necks of horses. They spoke in small foolish tinkling voices, they did not give tongue to thunderous awesome sounds such as this.

He took his first timid step inside the building. The thick walls, the queer openings, the wooden floors—everything frightened and confused him. He tried to remember that a boy of the Real People was always brave. Especially he did not want William Squirrel to know that his heart now raced with fear.

Before him in the hallway was a queer sort of thing, a series of little wooden shelves, one above the other. Suddenly Master Dawson appeared at the top of the shelves and began to walk down them. Wayah gasped. What an odd magic-like place this was. He wished he had never laid eyes on any white people.

Behind the master came a white woman. She too walked down the wooden ledges as though it were nothing unusual. Her long skirts swayed back and forth around her and made her look as though she were going to fall with every step.

Master Dawson laid his hand on the Wolf's shoulder. "Mistress Gough is the housekeeper for all the college, Wolf," he said slowly. "She will look after you now."

The woman gave Wayah a sharp look. Her eyes were hard and there were frown lines cut deeply into her forehead. She made him more afraid than ever.

"Come," she said and laid a bony hand on his shoulder. She steered him toward the stairs. Sweat broke out on him. He took a step upward and clutched the bannister. How could he walk on this queer thing? And what would happen when he got to the hole in the roof? Would he fall down on the other side? He clung to the newel post.

The woman pulled on him. "Come along!" she urged impatiently.

"The boy has never seen stairs before, Mrs. Gough," the master said gently. "Let the child take his time."

"Then he must take his time, not mine, Master Dawson," she answered briskly. "I've a deal to do this day besides help heathens up and down stairs." She marched up the steps, hauling the shivering Wayah behind her.

At the top of the steps Wayah was astonished to find another hall almost like the one he had left. Mrs. Gough pulled him down the hall and around to another flight of steps. At the top of this stair things seemed suddenly less strange to Wayah, in spite of being so far up in the air. The ceilings were low and sloping and the rough boards and plaster were something like the mud and log walls of houses at Chota.

In the single long room stood five queer looking contraptions, each standing on four firm legs. On top of each one lay a sack of straw.

"There," said the housekeeper. "That bed's yours, there by the window." She opened a small chest at the foot of the bed and took out some clothes, breeches, shirt, and stockings. "There's a blanket in here, though you'll likely not be needing it. Your shoes are under the bed. And this peg, here, is for you to hang your clothes on. Now quick, take off that wicked garment and put on some decent clothes. And when you've dressed, get yourself downstairs to Master Dawson. The College had ought to hire him an usher to take care of these things. It oughtn't to fall to my lot." She swished out of the room.

Wayah, who had barely understood a word of this, stood motionless where she had left him. After a while he moved to the window. The trees pressed up to it. How green and alive they looked. It might, after all, be pleasant to live high in the air like a bird. He put out his hand to touch them, but something stopped him—something that wasn't there.

He gave a little cry of fear and stared in horror at the glass pane. But then he remembered the sparkling covering he had seen over the windows. He had not known that one could look through it as easily as if it were not there. How could there be a thing you could touch but not see? What magicians the white men were! He was afraid of them, he couldn't help it.

He sat down on the bed. There were the clothes. He knew he was supposed to put them on. He touched them gingerly. It would be like taking off his old skin and putting on a new one. Once he was dressed in those clothes, he was no longer Wayah, a boy of Chota, but Wolf, a student at Brafferton Hall.

At last it was done. How the white man's clothes pinched and bound! The whites might be wonderful magicians, but how stupid they were to dress like this when they might wear simply a breechclout and be comfortable.

He pulled on the stockings. His legs felt hot and smothered in

the clinging cloth. But the shoes he left under the bed, for he did not see them nor had he comprehended Mrs. Gough's instructions.

Stiffly he sat on the edge of his bed. He did not know what was expected of him now. He was almost certain that he should go back to Master Dawson. But must he go down those steep wooden slopes by himself? Or should he wait for someone to get him? He stayed in the room, sweating in his new clothes. No one came.

At last he made up his mind. He was brave. He did not need to be sent for and led around like a child. He would find his way back to Master Dawson. He went to the stairs and looked down. The door at the bottom had been left ajar. He eased down and slipped out into the second floor hall. There was no one about. He edged along the railing to the top of the next flight of steps. Twice he put out his foot and twice he drew it back. His courage deserted him. It seemed such a curious way of doing things. He stood gripping the post with both hands.

Suddenly beneath him there was a sound of running feet. Then the redheaded boy appeared at the bottom of the stairs. He scurried up beside Wayah.

"Master sent me for you," he said, grinning. "And I was glad to get away. Greek verbs, ouch! You look fine, but I think this is the weather for a breechclout myself. Where're your shoes? Master'll raise Cain if he sees you going about in your stockings. Come along, they must be upstairs."

He ran the rest of the way up and disappeared into the Indian boys' room. Wayah could only stare.

In a minute the white boy came clattering back with the shoes in his hand. "Here," he said and pushed one onto Wayah's foot. "Get 'em on and we'll go down. Master's getting fed up with Grigley, he's sure to beat him in a bit and I don't want to miss it."

Wayah shoved his feet down hard and worked them into the stiff and horribly uncomfortable shoes. He had never before worn anything except moccasins. The Wolf bit his lip and remembered that he was brave. Holding to the rail he went awkwardly down behind the redheaded boy.

In the schoolroom Master Dawson was talking crossly to Grigley. The other boys were studying meekly, their eyes on their books, but Wayah felt certain they were listening closely.

The master broke off as his new charge came in. He led Wayah to a table near his desk where the four other Indians were seated. "I wish I could spend more time with you this afternoon, Wolf," he said, "but perhaps it is best not to rush you. William, show Wolf the speller. I must get back to my Greek scholars."

He went away and Wayah was left with the cruel-lipped Shawnee boy, who handed him an odd-looking flat box which fell apart into many, many leaves, all as thin as dried poplar leaves. Wayah understood that this was a book and the little black marks on the leaves, like so many ants, were the white man's talking marks. He listened with all his ears, but he heard nothing.

The other Indians paid him no attention. They took feathers and scratched on paper with them. And so the hot afternoon dragged by. Wayah thumbed back and forth through the book while his clothes pinched and chafed him and the boys' voices droned on and on. He was thirsty and hungry and wretched and in his heart he knew that this was worse than running a gauntlet or being tied over a slow fire.

The bell rang and the boys rushed outside, but Wayah sat at his desk, too miserable to move. The boys came back from the mid-afternoon break and the school went on. Every time the bell rang his insides knotted in terror. He could not get used to the bell. He did not see how the others could take it so calmly, that dreadful sound. It seemed to Wayah that it must be the voice of a powerful god which ordered the white men to do this and that. He was afraid not to obey it, but he did not know what it wanted.

When it rang again, the boys all stood up and there was something about them that made Wayah know the long day was almost over. They filed outside and this time Wayah went with them. They walked over to the big house and entered a room where a dim light shone on a gleaming cross set on a table.

William Squirrel showed Wayah where to sit. There was much jumping up and down and kneeling and singing. Wayah felt sure this had something to do with the white man's god. He couldn't really pay much attention. He could only crouch miserably in his place and once in a while put his hands to his aching head.

After a while it was over. The white boys went away. William Squirrel took Wayah to another big room where many men and older boys were getting ready to eat at long tables. The Indians with Master Dawson sat at a small table away from the others. Someone brought them bowls of stew and pieces of bread and mugs of something which smelled like rotted persimmons.

Wayah was hungry, but the sight and smell of the food made his stomach churn. He could not eat this stuff. He tried a bite of the bread but it stuck in his throat. He felt as though he were going to choke to death. He stood up and looked wildly around him. The hot room with its queer smells made him sick.

Master Dawson came quickly and led him outside. "Wait here on these steps," the teacher said.

Wayah sat and stared toward the setting sun, where it perched, big and red, on the distant line of black woods. Its bottom edge began to disappear. The soft hazy glow over the pasture dimmed. The cows and horses grazing there turned from rose to violet as twilight settled over the College of William and Mary.

It was cooler and very pleasant. The smell of damp earth and green things was sweet. Some of the feeling of sickness and strangeness began to go away.

The master came back and brought with him a mug of something hot and clear. "Drink this tea," he said and Wayah drank. It was strange tasting but soothing. He ate the corn cakes he was handed and felt much better.

Master Dawson went back into the dining hall. Wayah crept away to the Brafferton and up the dark steps to the Indians' attic room. He took off his clothes and put on his breechclout, still lying where he had thrown it across the bed. Through the window he could see the trees and a thin new moon climbing the evening sky. He came closer to peer out and bumped his head against the magic stuff you could see through. He recoiled a little and then put out his hand and touched it. It was smooth and cool as a mountain stone. Wearily he leaned his head against it and watched the moon mount higher in the sky.

- 5 -

The Winking Magic Stone

IN the night something woke Wayah. He didn't know what, for it was as black and quiet in the attic room as it would be at home. It wasn't the other Indians, they slept peacefully. He lay there thinking he must have been asleep for some time. Before the others had come up to the room he had settled himself on his bed and done a thing he knew how to do—withdrawn himself from his pain and worry and unhappiness into some deep place in his mind. Curled up he had gone easily to sleep, for he was very tired. He had only sensed the others coming in and lighting candles and talking.

Now he lay wakeful on his straw pallet. It was too soft. He preferred his hard cane bed at Chota. He turned restlessly and it rustled under him like a live thing. He twisted again, unable to lie still. He could not get back into the dark cave of sleep, the soft bed and the whispering straw kept him awake. Finally he rolled off his bed onto the cool floor. That was better. In a few minutes he was sleeping again.

The bell roused him. He scrambled up from the floor in fear and bewilderment. The other Indians were sitting up in bed, yawning and stretching. They began to dress hurriedly. William Squirrel went to a corner and poured water from a leather bucket into a bowl and washed his face with his one hand. The others simply began to pull on their clothes.

The Shawnee threw a glance over his shoulder at Wayah. "Dress!" he ordered in a harsh voice. Wayah understood. The voice of the god at the top of the house had commanded them all to rise.

He dressed as fast as he could. Still before he had squeezed his feet into his shoes the god spoke again and the others rushed down the stairs. He hobbled after them. At the foot of the stairs they waited at the door till Mr. Dawson opened it and let them out.

They marched once again across the yard to the chapel. Wayah was not so befuddled this morning. He sat with the other Indian boys and watched in amazement all the kneeling and rising, and heard the strange sounds of their singing—a wail such as wolves would be ashamed to make on a cold night. The table with its gold cross and embroidered cloth he thought very pretty.

Next, the god-bell ordered them back to the school room. Wayah sat at the table with the other Indians. His breeches pinched him, his legs sweated in the stockings, the edge of the bench cut his legs where they swung inches above the floor. But he did not wriggle or complain. He sat still and straight-backed. He was one of the Real People.

All the boys except Wayah went to the teacher's desk and took small knives and sharpened their quill pens. The teacher moved among the tables pouring a black liquid into little vessels. It was a terrible looking stuff and smelled worse. Wayah hoped he would not be given any for he did not think he could drink it. But the master poured a pot full and set it in front of him.

"Those students who are receiving instructions in penmanship, make a fair copy of the Collects for the day, also the Lessons," said Dawson. "Grigley, finish those sums I set you yesterday. Duncan—where is Duncan?"

"Here, Master," answered the redheaded boy.

"Ah, Duncan, you and Boatwright shall work upon Latin declensions this morning. There, in the corner, where I have placed the Grammar."

When he had dispensed these tasks, the master approached the table where the Indian boys sat. Three of them were busy writing. Wayah was relieved to see that the black stuff was not to drink. William Squirrel was reading a book and the master stopped and spoke to him about certain things in it. Then he went up to his desk and motioned Wayah to him.

The Wolf walked stiffly up to the desk and stood silently with folded arms, waiting.

The master smiled. "We are glad to have a boy of the Cherokees with us," he said slowly. "We hope to teach you many things. We want to teach you about our Lord and Savior, who dwells above and has instructed us to love one another."

Wayah understood. The bell-god on top of the house. The white men could do nothing, not even love, unless the god said they might.

"When you have learned your catechism and read your Bible, you will understand more of this," the master went on. "But first we must teach you your letters. And before that we must give you a name, a new name. For a Cherokee name is not suitable for a boy who is learning to become a Christian."

He pondered a moment. "Wolf is good enough, a good name. But for a Christian name—Adam! Adam it shall be for he was the first man created in God's image and you shall be the first Cherokee boy to be fashioned in God's likeness of a Christian life. Adam Wolf, do you understand?"

Wayah nodded. It was easy to change a name. It had happened to him before. It would happen often during his life so that by the time he became as old as Otonee, his grandfather, he would have used and thrown away a great number of names. It was, after all, only a name. It did not change his height or his legs or the color of his eyes.

"Adam Wolf," he said easily. It was a good enough name. It did not screw his mouth up like "William Squirrel," a name he would never have learned to live with.

"Now, Dawson went on, "we have no time to lose. You have much to learn. Quickly, now, back to your place."

So Adam Wolf spent the morning learning how to hold a quill pen, how to dip it in the black evil-smelling ink, how to make marks on paper. He made a great many marks he didn't intend, blots and splashes. Over and over again he tried to copy the letters the master had showed him. There were two kinds, big ones as straight and bold as warriors, and little ones which did much wiggling and jumping. But none of them made any sense to him, though obediently he struggled to do as he was told.

Once he looked up from his work to catch the eye of the red-headed boy, Duncan, upon him. Duncan grinned and made a horrible face, stretching his mouth wide and putting out his tongue to touch the end of his nose.

Adam stared. Did one learn also to do this in the white man's school? What possible good could it do? Would he ever be able to do it? Cautiously he spread his lips and reached out a curving tongue. It was hopeless. He would never manage.

The voice of the god bellowed again from the rooftop and it was time to eat breakfast. Wayah could not help thinking that he preferred the gods of his own village. They might instruct a hunter how to hunt but that was because the gods were in charge of the game. When a person ate or drank or slept or walked was his own affair, not the gods'.

At home people ate when they were hungry, not when they were told to. They scooped up a bowl of stew or cut a piece of bread or meat, whatever was left on the hearth for the family. That seemed the right way to Wayah. Surely his stomach knew more about this than the bell.

In the big building, the College, Adam sat with the other Indians and ate his porridge and bread. He was hungry and the food did not taste as strange as it had tasted last night.

At first he thought only about food. When he was nearly full, he looked up and about the big room. There seemed to be some more than ordinary disturbance. A man who looked almost exactly like Master Dawson came and went several times and there was a buzz of talk among the white boys.

Finally Master Dawson stood up and announced in a loud

voice, "A calamity has taken place. Doctor William Dawson, President of this College, has lost the great garnet from his ring. Anyone who has any knowledge of its whereabouts will kindly report the matter to one of the masters or to me."

He sat down and the white boys once again chattered and talked. William Squirrel turned to Adam. "You understand?" he asked. "A thing of much value is missing. Perhaps you stole it, Cherokee."

Adam went on eating. He had heard most of the words. Someone had lost a garnet. A garnet might be a horse of some very special kind. Or a musket with fancy decorations. Or a coat of green color with gold buttons. At any rate it was gone and he knew nothing of it.

The day wore on. Wayah tried hard to make sense of the little marks, to understand what the teacher said to him. He must do it, for his people's sake, he kept reminding himself. But sitting still in that hot room, with those foolish clothes on, took all his strength so that he hardly had any left over for studying. By the time classes were dismissed his head buzzed and swam and his legs hurt fiercely.

Perhaps this was what it felt like to be changed by the white man. The pains came from losing some of his Indian ways. His grandfather's words were true. He was being divided in two like an oak split by a lightning bolt and it wasn't pleasant.

Soon after supper the Indian boys were marched up to their room. Master Dawson came with them and brought a stub of candle which he lit and placed on the table in the center of the room. He also carried a blue coat with square metal buttons. It seemed very fine and handsome to Adam.

"Adam Wolf," said the teacher, holding up the coat. "Tomorrow is the Sabbath. On that day we go to church and to keep the day holy we wear our finest clothes. Here is your coat, Adam Wolf, to wear to church on Sunday morning. Mind that you keep it clean and whole."

He hung it up on one of the pegs in the wall. Then he opened the boy's chest and took out a hat and a very fine shirt with a ruffle. "These are yours, too. To wear to church."

He turned to William Squirrel. "See that he is properly attired on the morrow, Squirrel. And that his shoes have a polish. And I will attend to it that next week he has buckles for them and for his knees."

"Yes, Master," the Shawnee boy inclined his head.

Dawson went out and the boys were left alone. The four students stared at Adam, who looked away and sat uneasily on the edge of his bed. Nobody said anything, and by and by William Squirrel took up a book and began to read by the light of the candle. Wayah noticed he kept his arm stump in his lap in the shadows.

The two youngest boys sat on the floor and played a game of chance with some small stones. But the fourth boy suddenly shoved the straw mattresses from two of the beds and took the long cords, which served as springs, from the frames. Knotting them firmly together, he then tied one end of this rope to the bed under the window. The other end he lowered outside. He leaned out and listened for a long time. A quick glance below and he suddenly plunged through the window and down the rope. The bed pressed hard against the wall under his weight.

Adam ran to see what had become of the boy.

William Squirrel spoke up. "Go with him, Cherokee," he urged jeeringly. "You two are alike. That Saponi cannot sleep under a roof. After the master locks the door at night, he goes down the rope to run in the woods and sleep in the bushes like a fox." His face squeezed together in disgust. "He will never be anything but a savage. Go with him; Cherokee."

That would be good, Wayah thought sadly. To sleep where the air is fit to breathe once again. But he couldn't go. He was pledged to stay here, with the white people and their crazy ways and their god that crouched on the roof and their itching clothes. Even if it meant that he would die, he had to stay.

But perhaps some night he could slide down the rope. Just for a while. Only for a short while to be free once again, to be Wayah of the Real People in breechclout and moccasins. Wearily he climbed on his squeaking mattress and shut his eyes. He hoped his uncles knew what a dreadful place this was.

Next morning he changed his mind a little. Dressed in the ruffled shirt and the blue coat, he felt very fine indeed. The Saponi had returned in the night and the five Indians went below to join the older boys who boarded at the college. They marched off down the wide street behind the masters in their flowing black gowns and square black hats. Adam was glad he did not have to wear such somber clothes but could walk in the line in a handsome coat and hat.

Two by two they moved down the street. Wayah's head turned this way and that. His eyes felt as if they must pop from their sockets with all there was to see, the great houses with their flashing windows, the gardens of flowers and shrubbery, the people going here and there, clad in bright colors.

And the carriages! Wayah had heard of such, leather rooms pulled about by horses. It had not seemed to him a real thing, yet here they were. The great wheels that turned in dizzy circles fascinated him. Who would have supposed there were such things? Oh, the white men were great and wonderful people. Their magic was a powerful magic!

The churchyard was full of big white stones which interested Wayah, but he was not allowed to stop and see them. He was hurried into the church. Before him was a doorway hung with the skins of some animal. The animal was blue, a deep gleaming blue, and its fur was short and soft. With the others he passed through the hangings into a high-ceilinged light colored room which made him gasp with astonishment.

The students went up some steps onto a balcony. From here Adam could see everything. He almost cried out with surprise and excitement. The church was crowded with people. There were big windows all around which let the sun into the pale room so that the bits of gold here and there glistened and shone. On the floor below him people sat on benches enclosed in boxes. Adam had a glimpse of the redheaded Duncan and over there he spied Grigley and another of the town boys.

After a while the people began to sing. Master Dawson marched to the front of the church and after him came a man

with the most elegant clothes of all. He sat in a special chair with
a little roof over it. Wayah knew this must be Dinwiddie, the head
man. He felt a little thrill at seeing this great man.

There was more of the singing and jumping up and down. Master Dawson got up in a round wooden enclosure and talked. The
church became hotter and hotter and in his many layers of
clothes Adam sweated and grew restless. The college masters
looked at him sternly when he wriggled and he tried hard to stay
quiet.

At last it was over and they proceeded back to the college. Still
in their good clothes they went to the dining hall and ate some sort
of roasted fowl and many things which Wayah did not recognize.

At last Master Dawson told the Indians they might go into the
garden for an hour. "Remember this is the Sabbath," he admon-
ished. "No unseemly games or loud noises."

On the brick walks the boys moved up and down solemnly in

their finery. Adam's legs ached to run and run and run. William Squirrel spoke in English to the other three but he would not talk to Wayah. The Wolf was suddenly filled with longing for his home and his family. Forlornly he wandered around a corner of the Brafferton by himself. One of the older boys came hurrying toward him. Wayah stared.

"Out of my way, you little savage," yelled the boy crossly and gave the Cherokee a shove. In his binding clothes and his stiff shoes Adam lost his balance and could not regain it. With a cry he fell backwards into a patch of ivy, throwing his arms wide.

The fall did him no harm, but he feared for his new coat. He lay for a minute watching the white boy's retreating back. He hated that boy. He hated this school. He hated the white people. His hand clenched on the damp earth. His fingers touched something smooth and hard.

Adam scrambled to his feet and opened his fist on the thing he had found. It was oval shaped and polished, as big as a pigeon's egg, a stone of glistening, gleaming deep mysterious red.

Wayah's heart leaped. A magic stone!

- 6 -

Trouble

FOR the first time since he had arrived at the school Wayah smiled. He stood gazing down at the winking red stone in his hand. An amulet! The gods of his grandfather, the Long Person and the Ancient Red, had sent this magic to show him how they watched over him. Was it not as colorful and ever moving as fire? And as smooth and deep as the river?

It was a touchstone to keep him from being split in two by the white men. As long as he had it, the white men and their school and their queer ways could not harm him.

Wayah's fist closed tight on the stone once more. He glanced around him. No one was watching. Swiftly he pushed in among some bushes and slid along the wall of the Brafferton to the door. Then he darted inside and up the stairs.

Going to his chest, he took out one of the long worsted stockings and dropped the stone down into the toe. He placed the stocking at the bottom of the chest underneath all his clothes. It seemed to him a poor hiding place. Perhaps the magic stone would die shut away in the white man's box with all those smothering clothes.

But it would be safe there until he could think of a better place to hide it.

He wandered over to the window and looked out toward the south. What an empty place the sky was without the Cherokee mountains! Williamsburg lay under a big lump of nothing with a dark line of woods, a dry field or a strangely-shaped house all that you could see as you gazed around.

At home, Chota was the center of a blue and shadowed bowl, a bowl that held up the sky and gave it depth. The sun rose and set behind those old and lovely peaks, in summer the cloud shadows slid over them like water, in winter the snow made them glisten.

He sighed a little. At home now, on this sunny afternoon, the boys would be playing ball by the river. The crows would cry out from the corn fields where his mother and the other women would be working and singing. He turned away from the window abruptly. It did not do to think of such things. He was here at the white man's school to do a deed that must be done for his people. He would do it.

After a very skimpy supper, the Indian boys clumped up the stairs to their room. Their feet made a terrible noise. Why would anyone want to wear such things on his feet, thought Wayah, looking down at his black square-toed shoes with their thick soles? No one could be quiet in such things. No one could steal up on an enemy or a deer when his feet made a noise like thunder every time he stepped.

He was glad to take off his shoes and his Sunday clothes. He put on his breechclout and moccasins. But William Squirrel put on his school clothes and took up a book and began to read.

"It is because he can never be a real Indian, that he tries so hard to be a white man," thought Wayah, staring at the stump of the other boy's arm. For a second he pitied the Shawnee.

The two younger boys sat down on the floor and began their game again. They were Pamunkey boys from the same village, and they were fast friends.

"It must be nice to have a friend," thought Wayah sadly.

The two of them were just alike, small and thin and big-eyed. They coughed a great deal and Master Dawson worried about them and talked sometimes of sending them home. But they did not seem to mind being at the school or doing the work, as long as they could be together.

The other boy, the Saponi who had climbed down the rope, was Gideon Green Peach. He was about Wayah's age, lively and quick. He hated the school and the school work and he made it plain. Some days he seemed to work hard at his books. Other times he sat and stared sullenly ahead of him. Master Dawson might talk and cajole as much as he liked, the boy did not seem to hear. Even when the master slapped him on the shoulder with the ferule, he did not blink.

Now the Saponi came toward Adam. "Knife!" he said, holding out his hand. Wayah stared. "Give knife," he repeated fiercely.

Wayah shook his head. "No knife," he answered.

The Saponi grinned wickedly. "Get knife. Kill William Squirrel," he cried, making slashing gestures in the air as though he were cutting the Shawnee into little pieces.

William Squirrel laughed shortly. "The Saponi is a fool warrior," he told Wayah. "He thinks to kill all the masters and all the students. He thinks to lead his people in a war against all whites. The Saponis can no longer fight. They are women!" he ended scornfully.

Wayah shared his scorn. Everybody knew the Saponis were a beaten tribe whose warriors now spent more time stealing the white man's rum than trying to hunt or wage war. But he couldn't help sharing Gideon Green Peach's feeling too. Oh, how wonderful if all the whites would die and leave the Indians as they had been when his grandfather was young and no strange pale skins ventured near the country of the Real People.

But Gideon Green Peach was not taken aback. He kicked off his shoes and did a little stamping dance all around the room. There were holes in his stockings and one toe stuck out. Adam thought that soon there wouldn't be anything left of his stockings, the way he leaped about. He pranced by a window and stopped to look out. After a moment he ran and snatched up the leather bucket of water which was kept in the room in case of fire. He carried it quickly but carefully back to the window and waited. Suddenly he thrust the bucket outside and emptied its contents.

There was a sound of splashing and a howl from below. William Squirrel grunted and went back to his reading. The two little Pamunkeys looked at each other and chuckled. Adam sat down on his bed and watched. He did not know what would happen now.

In a little bit there was the sound of feet on the stair. Master Dawson unlocked the door and came up into the attic room, followed by one of the boarding students at the college. The boy's face was red with anger and his clothes were dripping.

The two Pamunkeys stuffed their pebbles hastily under the beds. Master Dawson did not approve of this game, especially not on the Sabbath. William Squirrel closed his book and stood up. Adam did too, though he didn't know why. The Saponi was curled up on his bed with his eyes shut as though asleep.

The Reverend Mr. Dawson looked around at them rather sadly, it seemed to Adam.

"One of you has thrown water out of the window upon young Randolph walking below," he said slowly. "I pray that the guilty one will own his blame. William Squirrel will no doubt tell me the name if I ask, but I prefer to have you act as honorable young men and confess your own faults."

William Squirrel looked grave. The two little Indians stared stupidly. Wayah cast his eyes to the floor. He was afraid if he looked at Master Dawson, the teacher would think he was the one.

"Young savages," muttered Randolph. "They ought not to be allowed here with gentlemen."

William Squirrel opened his mouth but before he could utter a sound, the Saponi bounded off the bed. "I pour water," he announced proudly. "I pour water on man like you pour it on William Squirrel, Master."

Reverend Dawson frowned. "What do you mean?" he asked impatiently.

The Saponi capered around the room, shooting sidewise glances at Randolph. "Bab-ba-tize! Bab-ba-tize!" he crowed.

"He means he saw you baptize me with water in the church," explained William. "He pretends that was what he was doing."

Master Dawson looked scandalized. "For shame, to make sport of a most holy sacrament," he cried, "to say nothing of the wicked wilfulness of spoiling Master Randolph's clothes. For this you shall

- 45 -

be punished. Now apologize to Master Randolph. And fetch a fresh bucket of water from the well."

"I sorry," Gideon said, adding a long string of Saponi words afterwards, his chest heaving with suppressed laughter.

Seizing him by the ear Reverend Dawson marched the Saponi out of the room. The student looked around at the Indian boys. "Brutes," he sneered and went out, squeezing water from the bottom of his coat.

Adam did not know what the word meant, nor did he care. But looking up, he caught a glimpse of pain in William Squirrel's eyes.

The days went very slowly. Gradually Adam was getting used to his stiff clothes and his pinching shoes. He learned to understand more English. The little black marks on paper began to speak to him. He was surprised to find that you could hear with your eyes. And yet was it not always so? The trampled grass, the broken twig, told him where the other boys had gone if he had to stay in the village to do some task and was late going out to play. Now these curious little marks also spoke in a silent voice and told him through his eyes what someone in another place had said and thought. Sometimes it seemed to Wayah a very marvelous thing.

He learned about the white man's God. He did not, after all, live on the roof. He lived in the sky, which was a proper place for Him to live. Adam saw the big bell that lived on the roof of the school and once he saw a man pull its tail and make it bellow. He knew now that the bell was used only to signal certain times, it had no life of its own. Yet it still seemed to him stupid that a man should eat when the sun stood at a certain point in the sky, regardless of whether he was hungry or not.

When Master Dawson read aloud to the Indians out of the book which the white man's God had caused to be written, Adam listened eagerly. It was a wonderful book which told of brave men and great battles, of a man swallowed by a huge fish and of rivers that parted to let the good people walk through but drowned their enemies.

There was another part which struck Wayah as extremely foolish. It was about a chief who was killed on a piece of wood, which the Cherokee thought a good and noble way to die, yet it seemed to make everybody, including Master Dawson, very sad. This chief said many things and some of them were wise, but some were foolish and light as a puff of air to an Indian boy. If you loved your enemies, how could they be your enemies any more? If you had no enemies, how could you go to war, how could braves prove themselves strong men?

Each school day he was Adam Wolf, sitting at the desk making small black marks with his quill pen. But as soon as the bell rang for a break in their studies, he was once again Wayah, the Cherokee boy, alone and lonely and far from home. The two Pamunkeys played by themselves, William Squirrel generally stayed indoors, reading or helping Master Dawson. The Saponi, before the bell stopped ringing, had climbed the fence into the pasture behind the school and started running like a mad thing, and did not stop till it was time to return to the schoolroom.

As for the white boys, they ignored the Indians. At Master Dawson's urging once in a while they would invite Adam to join some game. But he always refused. He would be awkward in his binding clothes. He did not want the white boys to laugh at him.

One day at the break Grigley organized the smaller boys into some sort of a game. Duncan watched for a few minutes. Then he shrugged and turned away, juggling something in his hand. Seeing Adam, he smiled suddenly.

"Come along, Wolf," he cried. "We'll play chuck-farthing together. I've a notion you'll be a master hand at it."

He led the way to a part of the yard where the grass had been worn away. Adam followed. He would not mind if just this one saw him fall in his stiff shoes. There was something friendly and kind about the redheaded boy's cheerful face with its many little dark spots called freckles. These seemed to Wayah as strange as the boy's coppery hair and his eyes that were as blue as chicory flowers.

However, the game Duncan proposed to play was not a running game. The white boy dug two holes a good distance apart.

Then he held out his hand and in the palm lay four shiny buttons, two brown and two black.

"You take these," he said, pointing at the brown buttons. "I'll take the black. You stand by this hole and try to pitch them in the other hole. It isn't hard."

It wasn't hard. Wayah had no trouble getting his buttons into the hole. It was almost too easy, but he was so glad to have someone be friendly to him that he didn't mind playing. He played all during the break with the redhead. Duncan hopped with admiration every time Adam's buttons spun neatly into the hole.

"I knew you'd be a master hand at this," he shouted.

And when the bell rang for studies to resume, he walked into the classroom side by side with the Cherokee, talking and laughing and flinging his arms about. Adam felt warm inside.

But later the Cherokee boy shook his head when Duncan urged him to join the ball game. He was afraid. Master Dawson saw him hanging back.

"Wolf," he scolded. "You must get some exercise. Running is good for boys. If you don't do some running, it may be that you will forget how."

Wayah's heart leaped in wild fear. Was it true? He stirred his legs under him. Had they forgot how to run? Swiftly he slipped away from the others and hurried up the stairs to his room. Oh, he might have known the white man's magic would work in some secret and terrible way. He might have realized that his arms and legs, encased in the white man's foolish clothes, would grow stiff and useless.

He went to his chest and rummaged among his clothes till he found the amulet. It was still alive. In his hand it shone and winked. Its color was as deep and vivid as ever. He stared at it a moment.

"Help me, help me!" he prayed to it. "Do not let my hands and arms and feet forget how to be an Indian boy."

He stood a few minutes filling his mind with thoughts of home, calling with all his strength on his grandfather's wisdom, on the essences of Fire and River, that they would help him. He was so far

away, so deep in thought that he did not hear the footsteps behind him until William Squirrel spoke in his ear.

"What are doing here, Cherokee?" he asked harshly.

Wayah whirled about, thrusting his hand with the magic stone behind him.

"What have you got? Give it to me," the Shawnee boy spoke threateningly and stepped toward Adam. "What are you hiding? Thief, you have stolen something!" He seized the smaller boy's arm in a fierce grip and began to twist.

- 7 -

"In the Gales"

WAYAH almost cried out with the pain. Biting his lip to keep back a moan, he squirmed to break William Squirrel's grip. But he was helpless. He went limp and then suddenly shot his elbow backward into the Shawnee's stomach. William Squirrel grunted and his grip relaxed.

In a second Wayah was loose, but the older boy lunged forward and pinned him against the wall. He began to slap Adam across the face and head with the stump of his arm, so that the Cherokee boy's head rattled against the timbers of the wall.

Red anger rose up in Wayah. The Shawnee might have but one hand, but he was big and strong. Wayah did not want to get into a fight. Still he would not give up his red stone and he would not be bullied by this Shawnee! He kicked out with one of the white man's heavy hard shoes and he heard the crack as his toe hit William Squirrel's shin. The other boy gasped with pain and stumbled backward until he sat on the floor, rocking and moaning as he held his leg.

Wayah fled. He clattered down the steps as fast as he could. He must hide his amulet quickly, quickly. But where? Should he dig a hole and bury it? No, he might never find it again. He had to hurry. The bell would ring soon. He must hide his red crystal before he went back into the classroom. It would never do to take it there, William Squirrel would surely make him give it up.

He slipped in and out of the bushes with his face screwed up with worry and thought. In this hole in the mulberry tree? No, a jay or a squirrel might steal it. Here under a bush? He walked on, shaking his head. One of the younger boys playing hide and seek would be sure to spy it. Where? Where?

He glanced all around. Something made him look up. William Squirrel leaned out of one of the attic windows watching him with a hateful face. Wayah scurried away down the path and behind one of the outbuildings.

He remembered then that one of the bricks in this building was loose. He had found it once as he had stood tracing with his finger the outlines of these curious stones that had aroused his wonder. The whole thing had been loose and he had worked it free in order to see all of it.

He found the brick. He stole quick looks here and there to be sure no one was watching. Then he slipped the stone out and pushed the amulet back into the cavity. In the back of the hole it gleamed with little lights and already he felt better. This was a much better and safer place than the bottom of his trunk. Here the stone could breathe and live.

He replaced the brick and wedged it in tight with a small twig. Now all was well and he smiled a little. When the bell rang, and he went back to the classroom, he gave William Squirrel a triumphant look.

The Shawnee sat at the table with his book open. But every now and then his hand stole down and rubbed the front of his leg.

That night after the others were in bed, Wayah got up and slid down the Saponi's rope. Silently he made his way to the school meadow and climbed the fence. His legs had not forgotten how to run. In his breechclout he sped round and round the field, leaping and jumping, running more swiftly than the deer. He could have outrun a rabbit. He could have outrun the Day Dweller across the sky. He stopped, panting, before the watching cows and told them what a great runner he was. They did not seem to care. He laughed and sped off once again around the pasture.

Later, when he climbed back up the rope, he gave thanks to the gods who had not let him forget to be an Indian boy. The blood ran hard and powerfully through his veins and it felt good. After that he went down the rope several nights a week to run and leap in the meadow and in the woods beyond it.

Now that he was almost sure the stone would protect him and not let him be split in two, he studied harder. Nothing he could learn from the white men would harm him too much, he thought. Besides, the little talking marks often said things that seemed to him most interesting. Much of it was foolish, of course, but some of it was amazing. Numbers were amazing.

At first, he had not understood about numbers. There were as many things as the number of fingers on his two hands, and more than that was a great lot and simply not worth bothering about. Soon, however, he saw the difference between twenty books and a hundred books. It was quite a great difference. If a war party came against your village with twenty men, it would not be so fierce a war party as one of a hundred men. Perhaps the white men were not so foolish after all.

Still, it seemed very stupid that every day should have so many names and numbers attached to it. Today was now, yesterday was gone and tomorrow had not come, why should you bother to put a name to any of them. Nevertheless he learned these names and numbers and when he practiced his penmanship he scrawled the date at the top of each page, as Master Dawson had told him to.

So Adam knew it was July 10, 1752, when the master announced that there would be a holiday in the afternoon. That day the master's brother, the head man of the college, was to be married. Master Dawson would perform the ceremony.

At first Wayah did not know what a holiday was. He could tell it was something good for the boys clapped and yelled. He did not want to ask William Squirrel. The master explained to Wayah that there would be no lessons that afternoon, that he was free to do as he pleased until the bell rang for evening prayer.

"You may go into the woods, or you may go into the town," explained Master Dawson, as Wayah hesitated by his desk after the others had left. "But you must be back at Brafferton Hall by the time the shadows grow long. Do you understand? And you must behave properly, as a young Christian gentleman should." He frowned a little.

Wayah looked straight at the master. He had grown used to Dawson's blue eyes and white face, they did not seem strange and unpleasant to him now. He liked the teacher who had tried to be kind to him and who could not help being a white man and thinking that white people had better notions than other people.

"I will be good, Master," said Wayah and smiled. The master smiled back. "I'm sure you will be, Adam," he answered.

Adam Wolf passed out of the schoolroom, debating. Should he be Adam Wolf and go into the town? Or should he be Wayah, one of the Real People, and take a path into the woods? It would be cool and quiet under the trees. Perhaps he could find a river to swim in.

But he had not yet been into the town. He longed to see more of it than he saw from his third story window. Much as he loved the woods, he had many days of his life still to spend there. He had best not pass up an opportunity to see Williamsburg. He would go into the town.

Later, as he stood at the edge of the college yard, staring down the long, wide street which ran through the town to its far limits, he did not feel so brave. What a hubbub on this Duke of Gloucester Street! People, horses, and carriages sped everywhere and made Wayah's head reel to watch. He did not know whether he dared go into the midst of such turmoil.

Every now and then he took a step toward those marvels which lay waiting, but each time he hesitated and stopped. Surely he would be trampled by horses and walked over by the people, or knocked down and run over by the great flying wheels of the coaches.

A small boy ran by rolling a hoop with a stick. It seemed to

Wayah a hard thing to do, to keep a round wheel of wood rolling in front of you as you might chase a small animal. It must take skill. He wondered if he could do it. The hoop-roller was barefooted and Wayah thought perhaps that helped. He himself had changed his shoes for moccasins and how gladly his toes wiggled about in the soft skin casing!

Suddenly among the pedestrians the redheaded Duncan appeared, wandering along the street aimlessly. He saw Wayah and waved. He dashed toward the Indian. "Hello, Adam!" he cried cheerfully. "Are you in the gales?"

Adam looked mystified.

"I mean are you full of merriment and fun?" Duncan explained. "A holiday always puts me in the gales. Believe me, every hour away from Latin verbs is a pleasure."

Adam Wolf smiled. He still did not quite know what Duncan's words meant, but he saw that the white boy shared his joy in being away from school for the afternoon. "No lessons!" he exclaimed. "Good."

"Are you going to explore the town?" asked Duncan. Wayah nodded. "Well, I'll go with you. There's heaps to see, and I can show it to you."

They left the college yard. A short distance down the sandy street some boys came running toward them. When they saw Duncan, they crowded around him.

"We're going to paddle down Archer's Hope Creek all the way to James River," cried one.

"In my pirogue," spoke another.

"You'll drown," answered Duncan briefly. "That dugout's full of holes. I took note of it last week."

"Come along, Duncan," the first boy begged.

The redhaired one shook his head. "My aunt'd be mad at me for drowning and spoiling my clothes," he grinned. "I'm staying here."

"With the savage?" asked the pirogue's owner incredulously.

"His manners are as good as yours, Palmer," answered Duncan.

Palmer's face plainly showed what he thought of that. He turned and ran off down a small side street. The others followed.

"Ha!" hooted Duncan. "We're well rid of them."

The Cherokee boy couldn't help wondering why the white boy had befriended him. It was his hair, he decided. The warm glow must have spread from Duncan's scalp to his heart and made him take pity on lonely Adam Wolf.

"I've three pennies for us to spend too," the white boy added. "My aunt gave them to me for learning a chapter of the Bible. Come along and we'll spend them in the apothecary's right yonder."

He tore off across the street. But Wayah waited for a pack train and two buckskin-clad traders to pass before hurrying after him. Then he stopped in front of the shop to stare at the signboard swinging there.

Oh, the white men were full of wonders. For here was a picture of a fine white horse with a long fluted horn springing from the center of its forehead. He had not yet seen such a horse in Williamsburg, but no doubt all such animals were kept for the Governor's use.

"The Unicorn has the best of everything," boasted Duncan and raced in the door.

Wayah went after him, but the smell almost sent him reeling back out. Duncan did not seem to notice, but it was dizzying to the Indian boy. Not just one smell but dozens, all of them strange, sharp, pungent, sweet, mysterious, sneeze-making, eye-watering.

The place was lined with shelves, laden with glass bottles full of fascinating looking things, with boxes and bags and small bundles of leaves and roots. The smells from these bundles were the strongest. The sweet smells came from the confections lined up on the counter.

Duncan was running up and down, crying out, "Here's Spanish licorice, it's good. And caraway comfits. But almond sugar plums are the best. And toffee."

The candies were made in many different shapes, some round, some square, some in sticks, and some formed to look like fish and dogs and stars. What were they for, Wayah wondered?

Duncan held out his pennies. "Two pieces of licorice and two of the brown sugar candy, some barley sticks and two of the almond

sugar plums," he reeled off to the man who had moved up behind the trays of sugar meats. "If you please, sir," he added politely.

Outside many people stared at the two boys as they strolled up and down the streets munching their sweets and gazing at everything. Wayah felt as though he had been put under a spell. The strange melting sweetness of this food seemed unbelievable to him. It was sweeter than honey or maple sap, and tasted different from anything he had ever eaten before. It was all so amazing, to be walking in the white man's town, to be seeing all these wondrous sights. It made his head swim.

He saw many shops and houses. Black men were working away at one of the houses, building walls of the red stone called brick. Wayah knew now that the white men made these stones and he wanted to see it done. He would have to ask Duncan to show him sometime.

They passed the Bruton Parish churchyard. Wayah stopped. "What are big stones?" he asked shyly. It was hard for him to speak English to Duncan. He had learned much and spoke easily to Master Dawson and William Squirrel, but he was timid with the white boys.

"They are gravestones," answered Duncan. "They mark the places where folks are buried."

Wayah was awed. What great chieftains must be buried here under these huge square white stones with their carvings of flowers and letters and human birds!

"Whites bury many things with chiefs?" he inquired. "Bury their horses, bury carriages and beds?"

Duncan chuckled. "Why in the world would you bury a perfectly good carriage?" he asked. "Come on, it's gloomy here. Let's go get a drink."

He ran down the street, dodging around some small boys playing marbles in the dust. Then he waited for Wayah and together they walked along till they came to an open green field, smooth and fresh in the bright sunlight.

"Over yonder's a pump where we can get a drink," Duncan pointed out. "The folks who own it won't mind. I'll race you there."

He ran and Wayah pelted after him. Even in his stiff clothes the Cherokee boy ran well and easily and he was drawing ahead of Duncan when he saw something that made him stop in his tracks. A fearsome beast, with huge horns roached back over its head and a bunch of long hair on its chin, came galloping toward him.

It was all he could do to keep from shrieking with fear. Rolling its eyes wickedly the animal came straight at him. Suddenly a girl appeared from behind a hedge, yelling shrilly. She ran up to the goat and seized a rope trailing behind it.

Duncan had long since reached the pump and was watching with a grin as the girl dragged the goat off, scolding it as she went. Wayah grinned too. "I was afraid," he confessed.

Duncan laughed. "Oh, a goat can be mean," he admitted. "Once, one of our billies butted me off a fence and well-nigh busted my head wide open." He began to pump.

Wayah had seen pumps before but he never ceased to marvel at the machine that drew the water up out of the earth. He bent and drank where the stream gushed forth.

"Hurry!" gasped Duncan. "I can't keep this up any longer. I'm about to perish of dryness myself."

Adam pumped for Duncan. The sweets had made both of them very thirsty and they drank again. Then they wandered off across the green.

"It's dull here today," complained Duncan. "I like it when Market Square is teeming with people selling things, horses or meats and vegetables. And it's a fine sight when the militia marches by looking fierce and dangerous. Once when there was a fair here I saw an African leopard tended by a black dwarf! It was wonderful. Look over there by the tavern. That must be a cock fight."

They scurried across the street and in among the men to watch for a little bit. But Adam thought it was dull. Elks fighting, now, that was a thing to watch as they slashed with their great antlers and their sharp hoofs. But birds! That was foolish. Even Duncan soon grew bored and they went on.

The afternoon passed too fast for Wayah. There was too much to see. They stared in windows at a man sewing, through doorways at men mending guns. They watched negro servants currying horses or sawing wood, and one was sharpening a knife at a wheel that went round and round. The white men did everything with wheels, Adam could see. There were whetstones in the Cherokee mountains, good ones, but flat and easily carried about.

The boys passed a huge building which Duncan said was the capitol of all Virginia. Adam wondered what a capitol was. At the Public Gaol a man stood with wooden planks around his neck and hands and pinned to his breast was a sign that said FORGERY.

Duncan said the prisoner had made money and it was a crime. Adam's head was too full of marvels, it buzzed from too many strange sights, to puzzle this out. He followed the white boy down one street and along another. At last Duncan said he had to go home and do some work. Duncan's real home was on a plantation a good distance out in the country. But in order to attend school he lived in Williamsburg with his aunt.

"My aunt doesn't like me to be on the streets after five o'clock," Duncan said. "And it will not be too long before chapel prayers. You had better go back to school, Adam."

The Indian boy nodded. The shadows were lengthening. "You come to Chota sometime," he said. "I will show you my town."

"I'd like that," Duncan agreed. "Show me how to shoot a bow and arrow and let me go on the warpath."

"Yes, and hunt buffalo far to the west," added Wayah.

"I've never even seen a buffalo," Duncan mused. "Hunting and fighting, what a great life it must be."

Wayah smiled. "Yes," he answered. "But here is many things to see." And it had been exciting and much more fun with a friend to show it to him.

"You'd better hurry on," Duncan urged. "Straight down this street is the college. Farewell." Before he hurried toward his own house he watched a minute as the Indian boy edged along the street, his clubbed hair bobbing behind him.

Just ahead of Wayah was an elegant coach swaying along on its bright gilded wheels. A Negro man rode on top driving the horses. Wayah trotted behind it, intrigued, unmindful of the dust it threw up. Suddenly the coach stopped and the driver got down. Opening a door he took out a box and went into one of the buildings.

Adam stopped beside the carriage. It was painted and though the colors were faded, it was still very pretty and gay. For one quick moment he thought as a white man and understood that nobody would want to bury such a wonderful possession forever in a grave with the dead.

He touched the handle of the door and it swung open. He peeped inside. How grand it would be to sit in the little room and ride. He stepped up and squatted on the floor, feeling the leather seats and the cloth cushions. He glanced all around. He didn't see anyone watching. Cautiously he raised himself and sat on the edge of the seat. Then he leaned back and settled himself comfortably. If his family could see him now!

All at once there were loud shouts and a sharp sound as some one smacked the horses. The coach jerked forward. Wayah's mouth flew open. He sat up and leaned out the window. The ground was flying beneath him. He was terrified. He clutched the door post and somebody shouted his name.

"Have a good ride, Friend Wolf."

It was Grigley.

- 8 -

Worries and a Sign

THE coach gathered speed and rocked down the street, creaking and rattling. One door flew open and banged shut. A man ran alongside and grabbed at the trailing reins, yelling "Runaway! Runaway! Lookout!" The horses thundered on through the town, their heads tossing wildly, the harness flapping.

Inside the carriage Wayah was flung back and forth, from side to side. He grasped at the leather seats, at the floor, at the door, at anything at all, but the swaying coach sent him racketing around like a stone in a gourd rattle. He was frightened half out of his wits and his nose was bleeding.

Suddenly the horses swerved sharply to one side. The coach tilted dangerously as it bumped over the rough ground. Wayah bounced up, cracking his skull against the roof. He thought he was going to be sick. Grabbing frantically at the window frame he held on as hard as he could.

The horses slackened their pace. Adam crouched at the door trying to turn the handle. He must jump out now while he had the

chance. One of the back wheels began to wobble and then went shooting away from the carriage. The coach lurched to one side, there was a loud cracking noise, Wayah's door flew open and the boy went flying out onto the sandy street. He hit with a thud. The breath was all out of him. There was nothing in his chest but a hole with ragged gasping edges that burned like fire. Lights swam before his eyes and darkness hovered over him. He thought he must be dying.

But after a second his lungs began to fill with wind once more and his head cleared. He knew he couldn't lie there in a heap. He had to get to his feet and get away. The town people would say he had tried to steal the coach and would torture him without mercy.

He forced his eyes open and sat up. He was on a small street with no houses near him. A few yards away sat the coach, twisted to one side where the wheel was missing. And beyond it Wayah could see the rear wheel spinning madly along by itself. How big and strange-looking it was. Where would it go now that it was no longer a slave of the carriage?

The wheel began to swing slowly out in a wide curve and Wayah saw the terrible eye in its middle. It turned around and suddenly came whirling back straight at him! He stiffened with fright. It was coming to get him. There was nothing the white man's wheels couldn't do. It would be awful to be in their power.

With a scream he leaped to his feet and sped away. Somebody shouted after him. But he did not stop. He pelted on, dodging among the bushes and along paths and through high weeds till he came to a small stream.

He stopped in terror. He was lost. He had no idea where he was or even where he had run from. The shadows were getting long. He was lost, lost, lost, and Master Dawson would be angry. He had to find the college.

He was tired and hungry and scared and the thought of food and a bed, even the white man's bed, filled his heart. And he was NOT running away from the school. He did not want his teacher to think he was running away. He would not do a cowardly thing like that. He had to get back to the college quickly.

He turned and ran back the way he had come, searching for some familiar sign. Someone came toward him, a man on horseback. Wayah dodged quickly into the bushes. He didn't know why. It was simply that he was afraid.

With thumping heart he crouched among the arrowwood and little hornbeams till the horseman had passed. It gave him time to collect his thoughts. He was behaving like a fool. A Cherokee boy did not get lost. He had better sense. If he took the time and made the effort, he could find Brafferton Hall, he knew.

He came out of the bushes and tottered along the road until it divided. He took the upper road. When he thought he had gone far enough, he cut across a field and stood on a fence, peering in the direction he thought the school lay. Sure enough the tall brick chimneys were there. He scuttled through another field and a garden and there it was.

He raced across the road and through the grounds of the college. He was too late. He had missed prayers. Master Dawson would be angry and would not trust him to go to town alone again. He ran harder than ever and was relieved to see the other Indians loitering on the steps of the Brafferton. Puffing and panting, Adam went to stand with them.

William Squirrel gave him a scornful look. "It is lucky that Master Dawson has not yet dressed, even though the bell has rung for prayers," he said disdainfully. "He would not be proud to see you. What a dirty face! Go quickly and wash."

Adam was delighted to wash his hot face and hands in the cold water and take a long drink of its sweetness. He ran his fingers through his hair and straightened his clothes. In the twilight he looked presentable enough, and Master Dawson hardly glanced at him when he hurried from his quarters to lead the way to the chapel.

Wayah had trouble keeping awake during prayers and supper. But after he was in bed, he worried. Someone would be bound to tell. Someone must have seen the Cherokee boy in that fine carriage which had run away and broken itself in the dusty street!

That night he dreamed he was back in Chota. He saw his grandfather running toward him, very fast. When Otonee came close, Wayah saw he had no legs, but instead great round wheels that turned smoothly under him. It was horrifying.

The class had no sooner settled themselves at their desks the next morning than there was a knock at the front door. The boys pretended to go ahead with their work, as they were supposed to do, but Wayah's eyes slid toward the open classroom door. He saw William Squirrel's hand falter and stop with its quill pen, and he knew the other boys too were waiting to see who their visitor was. They all welcomed anything that kept the master out of the room and gave them a few minutes to forget their tasks.

Master Dawson had stepped out into the hall to the front door. Suddenly he returned to the schoolroom and Adam's heart gave a leap into his throat. Beside the master walked the Negro man who had been driving the coach which had run away with Wayah.

Adam sat very still. He wanted to think he had not been seen in the coach. But why would the coachman be here if he had not seen a Cherokee boy climbing up on those leather seats?

The coachman was an elderly man with gray hair and a stern face. His eyes moved over the faces of the boys as though he was searching for someone. Wayah thought about crawling under the desk, but he did not think it would do any good.

"Young gentlemen," said Master Dawson sternly, "yesterday in town a very fine coach was badly damaged and two fine horses frightened and exposed to the risk of great hurt. There is reason to believe that some boy from the school is responsible for this wrong doing. I hope that anyone who knows anything about it will come forward with his information.

The coachman looked straight at Adam Wolf. The Cherokee hung his head. Oh, how could he tell the master that he had only climbed up to see what the coach was like inside? No one would believe him if he said Grigley was responsible. Oh, oh, oh, he would be sent home, a wretched failure, and his mother's brothers would despise him for having failed his people. They would get no guns and they would die of hunger.

Who would have thought just climbing up to look inside one of those wheeled boxes would lead to so much trouble? He wished he had his red stone to hold in his hand.

"Yes, Grigley?" said Master Dawson.

"Please, sir," said Grigley smugly. "I saw it all. It was the new Injun, the Cherokee, who ran off with the coach."

Wayah went on looking down at the desk. He did not want to see Master Dawson's face. He could feel everyone staring at him.

Then the coachman spoke out. "You, boy. You ain't the only one who saw what happened. Maybe it was an Injun in the carriage. But I was watching from inside the house. I seen who untied the reins and smacked the horses to make 'em run. And it was you!"

Adam looked up in surprise. The coachman stood with a long finger leveled at Grigley.

"Master, no. He lies!" cried Grigley furiously. "I saw the whole thing. It was the Injun."

The coachman shook his head. "The Injun clumb up where he had no business to be, sir," he told the master. "But it be that boy there that done the mischief."

The teacher frowned. "Once too often, Grigley, you are at the scene when some unpleasantness takes place," he said severely. "I will see that your father learns of this and he shall set your punishment. But in the meanwhile you will keep your place at the breaks for next week and spend the time translating the day's Collect into Latin. That is your punishment for lying and trying to involve another person."

He turned to Wayah. He was still frowning and Adam Wolf would have given a great deal to get up and run out the door. "As for you, young Wolf," the master said gravely, "I am disappointed in you. You should know enough to stay away from other people's property by this time. You will not be allowed to go to town again until I have decided that you have learned this lesson. Hold out your hand."

Wayah did as he was told and the master struck him briskly six times across the palm with the ferule. Wayah had seen the other boys disciplined in this way and he knew that some of the younger ones had to struggle not to cry out. But such blows could never make a Cherokee flinch. He hardly felt the ferule.

Adam had expected much worse punishment. He glanced up at Master Dawson and suddenly the teacher smiled at him. "I will try to arrange for you to ride in a carriage sometime soon, Adam," he said kindly, and walked away with the coachman.

The boys went back to their tasks and Adam gave a sigh of relief. But in his heart he wondered about Grigley. Would he try some other devilment now that this had failed?

As soon as Wayah saw the President's new wife, he knew she was a witch. He had already suspected that she had great powers, for one of the boys had said she was a twin. When she came to eat a meal at the College Hall, Wayah saw she was left-handed. Otonee had always told him that left-handed people were witches. Wayah stared fearfully at her smooth black hair and white face as she talked and smiled with the teachers. A witch! He was a little frightened.

And he was right. Within ten days President William Dawson was dead. Everyone said he had died of a fever, but Adam Wolf knew better. The witch had killed him. All the students at the college marched in the funeral procession and Wayah saw the widow riding in a coach, pretending to weep. He hoped she did not see him. Her glance could only bring evil and pain to him.

The funeral was interesting to Adam, but the white men talked too much. They talked all the time. After the President's death there was again much talk of the President's lost garnet and how it should have been found before he died, since he had been so fond of it, and how if it was found now it would belong to Master Thomas Dawson, his brother.

Wayah heard that a reward had been offered. He had some vague notion of what a reward was and he thought perhaps he would like to have it. But how could he find and return the President's garnet. He did not even know what it was shaped like.

"What garnet like?" he asked Duncan cautiously.

"Oh, it's a good big one," answered Duncan. "It fell from its gold setting, you know. I wish I could find it. Seven shillings reward!"

Wayah said nothing. Duncan hadn't been much help.

Master Dawson grieved for his brother. At least Adam supposed he did, for all during the rest of July he seemed sad and some days bad-tempered. The weather was very hot. Adam found it hard to sit still in his clinging stiff clothes. He stared out the window, dreaming of the cool forests and the river at Chota. But Master Dawson's sharp voice recalled him to his hard seat where he wriggled in his scratchy shirt.

The boys were all restless and Master Dawson dealt out numerous smacks with his ferule during the long sticky afternoons. Wayah wondered if his uncles knew what a hard thing they were demanding of him.

August was even hotter, yet Master Dawson seemed to have a change of heart. At any rate he did not drive them so hard, he was less easily roused to harsh words, and some very hot afternoons he even dismissed classes and let the boys go out into the gardens and fields.

Adam welcomed these times. He and Duncan wandered and played together then, a thing they did not often do at the regular breaks. For Wayah was still shy about playing with the white boys. Besides, Grigley never missed an opportunity to trip him up, to kick him in the shins or gouge him in the ribs.

Even in the classroom he had learned to watch out for Grigley. Once when Wayah had been passing out copybooks, Grigley had jabbed his quill pen deep into the Indian boy's hand. Adam had smothered his cry of pain and wiped away the blood with the tail of his shirt. But he and Grigley were enemies and nothing would change that ever.

Some days Wayah would persuade Duncan to leave the playground games and run or wrestle with him away from the others. At such times Wayah thought how good it was to have a friend. Then in September Duncan was called home because his mother was gravely ill. Adam missed the redheaded boy. He missed his friend so much, in fact, that he began to worry about it.

Was it right to like this white boy such a lot? Otonee would not approve. And was it right to demand that Duncan leave the others to play only with him? His grandfather would certainly scold Wayah for this. A Cherokee was generous at all times, sharing his friends freely as he did his food and possessions.

Wayah groaned. He was becoming more and more white, not only in his relationship with Duncan but in other ways too. He no longer found his bed too soft. His stomach demanded food at the hours set by the white man. It was no longer awkward for him to eat with a knife and fork. He pulled on his clothes in the morning, even his shoes and stockings, without a thought to their strangeness.

And his studies, though they often seemed dull and hard, were not the foolish things he had thought at first. Especially the many ways you could use numbers. Numbers fascinated Adam, but he was ashamed to admit it. For numbers seemed to him a thing white men had invented and which they thought too much about.

Sometimes on those nights when the Saponi lowered himself out of the window, Wayah followed. He stopped in the yard beside the outbuilding and took out his magic stone and held it tightly.

Was it working? Was it keeping him from splitting in two? He frowned to himself in the cool damp fall night. He had felt no pain. He seemed to be the same person he had always been, and yet he was not.

He wished he could go home, if only for a few days. Or if Two Sticks would come to Williamsburg, to see how hard he was trying, how much he suffered. He laid his face against the rough bricks, longing for home, for a sight of his mother and father and their hut, for the sound of the river and the sweet dusty scent of burning leaves on a fall hunt.

But, no. He must not think such things. He had come here to do a task that had to be done. He would do it no matter how it affected him. In the dark he pressed the stone against his heart.

"Help me," he whispered. "Do not let me cease being one of the Real People."

Duncan was gone for some weeks, until his mother was well. When he returned, Master Dawson kept him busy all day long. Duncan was a good scholar, quick at his books when someone kept after him, but inclined to be lazy. Now Master Dawson was driving him to finish his work and not wait till the end of Trinity Term.

Early November was bad, wet, and windy. At the breaks the boys could seldom go outside. They stood about the halls and classroom in gloomy little groups. Adam stayed with the other Indians. He did not go to talk to Duncan, though he longed to. He even tried to be a little more friendly with William Squirrel. Since the two boys had fought over the stone, Wayah had avoided the Shawnee, who made no attempt to conceal his dislike. But as the weeks went by, somehow their quarrel began to die. They were together all the time, and it was hard for Wayah to remember to be angry with anybody all the time.

Master Dawson was always asking Squirrel to help Wayah with one thing and another. Teaching the Cherokee seemed to please the older boy and make him feel superior, and he no longer sent spiteful looks at Adam Wolf over the top of his books. Instead he spent many hours telling his pupil lots of things Wayah did not care to know.

Wayah hoped Squirrel would never truly be his friend. He would rather have Duncan.

One day he looked up and found the redheaded boy grinning at him. Wayah grinned back. "If I was a white boy," he thought, "we could be the best of friends all the time."

No sooner had he thought this than he was filled with panic. What a terrible thing! He must be turning white or he couldn't have had such a treacherous thought.

That night he lay long awake. Outside the wind roared in the big trees, drafts scuttled across the floor to keep them all from sleeping. Staring out into the stormy blackness Wayah prayed with all his strength to the Long Person and to the Ancient Red. He sent his mind out to the brick wall, to his magic red stone, which held their spirits. He looked far down into its moving fiery depths and prayed to the River and the Fire.

"Send me a sign that I am still one of the Real People," he begged. "Let someone come here to speak to me, in my own tongue, so that my ears will not forget. Let me hear the speech of the Cherokee once again."

Two days later Wayah looked up from his multiplication table to hear a sound that almost made his hair stand up with excitement. In the hall someone was speaking, and the language they spoke was the language, sweet as honey, soft as water, of the Cherokee.

- 9 -

The Wrong Kind of Cherokee

WAYAH half-rose from his seat. His quill pen slipped from his fingers. Oh, oh, oh, he could still understand, he was still one of the Real People, their tongue was still his tongue!

What was more he felt almost certain this was someone come to take him home. Two Sticks or Otonee or even Old Hop, the Emperor of Chota himself—someone had decided that Wayah the Wolf had done enough, that he had suffered sufficient heat and itching and loneliness and bewilderment.

Now they were coming to get him. They would say to these Englishmen, "Here is a boy, a hero, who has come to your school and learned your foolish ways. He has kept his part of the bargain and now you must keep yours. Return our son to us and give us guns and goods to show your good faith."

The voices were at the door. Master Dawson stood up, the scholars raised their eyes from their books. A man stepped into the room.

His shirt and breeches were white man's clothes, but on his feet were ankle high moccasins of softest white leather, tied with silk tassels. His face was tattooed with a pattern of black and blue dots, brass rings dangled from his ears, and in his scalplock stood a tuft of red deer hair.

After him came a woman, dressed in a long blue robe caught at the waist with a red girdle. She wore a great many ornaments, metal brooches and shining bracelets and numerous strings of white beads, and her cheeks were painted with vermillion. A small boy held her hand.

Behind her came other Cherokees and a white man. They were all talking excitedly but Wayah did not need to hear the name "Great Tellico" to know that these were the wrong kind of Cherokees and that no friends of his stood crowding at the door.

The white man came toward Master Dawson, holding out his hand. "John Watts," cried the teacher. "What a time since I've last seen you! How fare you?"

"I'm still alive," answered Watts. "Though it's a wonder, considering how long I've been living in the wilderness. Sometimes I reckon that white and red are so intent on scalping one another there soon won't be anybody left, not even a poor interpreter."

He turned back to the Indians. "Here is Ammonscossittee, Emperor of the Cherokees, with his wife and some members of the Great Tellico council and their wives. They are Governor Dinwiddie's guests and he has asked that they be shown the Indian school."

Wayah sank back in his seat. He looked scornfully at Ammonscossittee. What right had he to call himself Emperor of the Cherokees? He looked very young and Wayah doubted that he was more than twenty-three or -four. It was said that this so-called Emperor had never been on the warpath in his life. Great Tellico had no claim to being the main town of the Cherokee Nation, and having such a foolish and untried warrior as its headman was enough to prove what an upstart town it was.

Everyone knew that Chota was the mother town of the Cherokees. In its council house burned the eldest sacred fire, from which all the other council fires had been lit. The men of Great Tellico were jealous of Chota's power over the affairs of the nation and they were trying to steal it. Especially they wanted control of the trade with Virginia.

Adam seethed with rage as he watched how respectfully Master Dawson shook hands with the Emperor and how grave and courteous he was as he bowed to the Empress. His voice rang with pride as he said what a great privilege it was to have such a high-ranking personage visit his school. Wayah longed to tell his teacher what a mistake he was making to let this false Emperor impress him.

The master was telling the visitors that the whole building was for the use and education of Indian boys of any tribe in the Thirteen Colonies or of the lands to the west.

Ammonscossittee interrupted in a haughty voice. "Why are there white boys here?" he asked. "What right have all these white skins to the Indian's place?"

Watts translated this and Dawson hastened to explain. "Oh, how I wish it was filled to overflowing with Indian boys. But unfortunately many of the tribes are reluctant to send their boys to the school. So I am forced to take white students in order to fill up my time and earn my living."

When he heard this, the Emperor grunted. "Ha! I will send many boys from Great Tellico to school here," he exclaimed. "The Virginians are my friends. I trust them. I trust my children to their care, for I know they will be treated well. In return, the Virginians can send some of their sons to me and I will see that they are taught many great and useful things."

Wayah thought this was a good idea. True, the Cherokees had no such wonderful stuff as glass, nor could they make the little marks that talked. But they had much to teach—the mysteries of the encircling seasons, the songs to bring dead game back to life, how to fight bears, how to move silently and without a trace through the forests.

In the Indian villages white boys would not feel strange and lonely as Wayah felt here. At Chota and even at Great Tellico life was gay and easy and free. There was no clock-time to make the days and nights miserable. No one need ever feel knotted up on the inside and scratched on the outside with all the different things he must do or must not do.

Mr. Watts evidently did not think it was such a good notion however. He did not tell Master Dawson that part of what the Emperor said.

"Oh, splendid, splendid," cried the teacher when he heard that many boys would come from Great Tellico. "We already have one Cherokee boy here. Adam Wolf, stand forth."

Adam stood up and then the master beckoned him over. "Here is Adam Wolf, a young Cherokee lad who has been with us for several months," he told John Watts. "He came to Brafferton Hall like a worm out of the earth, naked. He has been clothed and fed and I have endeavored mightily to fill his mind and spirit with the goodness of Christian teachings."

The Emperor spoke directly to Adam. "Where are you from, boy?"

"Chota," answered Adam.

"Chota!" Ammonscossittee's eyes narrowed. "What are you doing here?"

Wayah was certain the Emperor knew why he was at Brafferton. However, Adam was not going to tell him what he already knew. After a moment's thought, he answered in English. "I am here to renounce the devil and all his works and the pomps and vanities of this world; and to learn the articles of the Christian faith and to try to keep God's Holy Will and Commandments."

At this Master Dawson looked enormously pleased and proud, the Emperor frowned in anger, and John Watts struggled not to burst out laughing.

"Boy, have you forgot your own tongue?" snapped Ammonscossittee.

"He says he came here to learn the Christian religion," translated John Watts hurriedly. "Some of the things he says are hard to put into Cherokee. He means no harm."

The Emperor looked around the room as though the whole subject now bored him past endurance.

"Would you like to see the rest of the building?" Watts asked quickly. "Master Dawson, show us everything you have to offer the Indian boys."

"Oh, gladly, gladly," cried the teacher. "Come along, right this way."

In all the months Adam had been at the school he had only twice gone into Dawson's study and never in any of the rooms on the second floor. He was anxious to see these but not with this group of Cherokees. However there was no chance to escape. The teacher grabbed him by the shoulder and guided him through the doorway.

The Indians squeezed out behind him. But out in the hall, Dawson suddenly turned and went back into the schoolroom. "Wait," he called to Watts. "I neglected to assign some of my scholars their tasks and they are in no great need of any extra holiday."

When he had gone, the Empress spoke suddenly to Wayah in a soft pleasant voice. "Do you like it here? Are you well-treated?" she asked.

"Yes," Adam answered.

It was true. To live in Williamsburg would not be a thing he did of his own choosing. But there was great magic and excitement here. He was glad of the many things he had seen and learned. And Master Dawson was a good and kind man, he liked his pupils and they liked him.

It was true that the white man's clothes were poor silly things, his bed was a foolish contraption, and his clock was an utterly useless invention. Nevertheless Wayah felt that he had been well-treated, sheltered, clothed, and fed. Some of the boys complained constantly about the food, which they said was all old turnips, meal after meal, with only a few new turnips added. Often Wayah longed for a piece of deer meat, but the breads and porridge and vegetables did not seem to him as strange as he had expected.

Master Dawson returned and crossed the hall to unlock the door to his study. "Welcome to my home, ladies and gentlemen," he said in his whispering voice.

The Cherokees pushed in. The Empress sat in the upholstered chair, the Emperor preened himself in the gilt-framed looking glass. The fireplace in the corner fascinated some of the braves, one even squatted to peer up the chimney, despite the low fire on the hearth.

Dawson opened the door into the next room. "Here is my bed chamber," he said.

The Cherokees without hesitation entered the room and tried

the bed, took Master Dawson's clothes from the hooks and pulled out the drawers of the dresser. They opened books, leafed through them, and then dropped them to the floor.

Adam was ashamed. But then he was ashamed of his shame. Was this not the way he himself would have acted six months ago? Like William Squirrel he was coming to take on more of the white man's ways than he would have thought possible.

The desk top was littered with chewed and broken quills and the inkstand had been overturned and the black stain not even sopped up. A great many papers lay about on the desk and some had been wadded up and thrown to the floor. A brave picked up these and smoothed them out and puzzled over the inked words on them.

There was something sad and lonely about that room and Wayah was glad to leave. They all mounted to the second floor. Master Dawson selected a key from a great many on a brass ring and unlocked a door. Wayah felt a little prickle along the back of his neck. He had never before seen this door opened. Gideon Green Peach had told him that this room was used by the white men to imprison evil spirits. He claimed to have seen strange lights flickering inside it at night when he slid down his rope. And once he had seen a huge mouth like a fish's mouth pressed against the window glass.

Adam did not believe that the master was going to show his visitors any imprisoned bad spirits, so he stepped into the room as eagerly as the others, for he longed to see just exactly what was there. He was disappointed. There were a few chairs and tables and a stand of shelves with a great many books with "Brafferton" stamped along the spine in gold letters. The dusty, musty smell was the smell of old books and closed air, nothing else. He didn't see any big fish.

"Our library," announced Dawson.

Over the fireplace hung a portrait of a pleasant-looking man with a great deal of long curly hair.

"That is a picture of Mr. Boyle, the man who has given the money for this school and for all the food and clothes and books which are given to the Indian students," explained Master Dawson.

The Indians stared. A warrior standing next to Adam Wolf spoke to him. "This man, he is here?"

Wayah answered. "No, he does not live here, but across the Great Waters."

Several of the braves murmured at this and turned away. Wayah knew why. They felt uneasy looking at this very lifelike image of a man. Perhaps the picture was seeking a soul and might take theirs.

"What do they say?" the teacher asked him.

Adam did not want to tell the master what really troubled the Indians. "They say the picture is very real," he answered at last. "Very like a man."

Master Dawson looked pleased. "I'm assured it's a very good likeness."

Wayah glanced up again. Perhaps so. The picture was a dead thing, he would rather look at a living man.

Across the hall was another locked door. Master Dawson opened it and stood aside to let the Indians in. There was another corner fireplace, but the only furnishings were two beds. The windows were curtained. This was the infirmary. Just the day before both the little Pamunkeys had been in here, recovering from yet another feverish coughing spell. Gideon said they would die before three moons had passed.

The interpreter explained about the shelves of bottled medicines and the paper packets of powders.

"Cherokee never sick," a chief spoke in broken English. "Sweat much."

Wayah nodded in agreement. The sweat house was a very good medicine, he reckoned. Better than that was wearing the proper clothes and eating and sleeping when you were hungry or tired, not by the clock.

There was another small room beside the infirmary but the Reverend Mr. Dawson said it was being used as a storeroom since the fireplace had a faulty flue. He did not open that door but passed on up the stairs to the third floor.

"Here is where the Indian boys sleep and study," Thomas Dawson said. "And they have a fine view from the windows in all directions. That is Adam Wolf's bed and chest there."

There was a note of pride in the teacher's voice. It surprised Wayah. He had not known that Master Dawson thought so highly of his Indian boys and what he could give them.

The Empress went to the window and looked out. "To live here would be like being a bird," she said. "It is high and there are trees around."

"But it is not like being a bird," Wayah wanted to tell her. "There are long cruel days of hardships and suffering and nights of such loneliness as to seem never-ending. Yet, I am a Cherokee boy from Chota, with the heart of the fierce mountain panther, and I am not afraid to live here and do what is asked of me. I doubt if the boys from Great Tellico could do this thing."

John Watts laid a hand on the Empress's arm. "Come, we have seen it all," he urged. "We have other things to do." Turning to Dawson, he said, "The Governor has invited the Cherokees to go to the theatre with him tonight. It is to be quite an occasion, and they must have enough time to prepare."

Master Dawson broke into a smile. "Why, my wife and I plan to attend the playhouse tonight. And young Wolf shall go with us and with his countrymen. He will be glad of their company, I know. And I'm glad of the opportunity to show him some more of our city. Oh, I am pleased!"

When Adam returned to the schoolroom, he found it hard to settle back to his books. He kept staring into the fire crackling in the fireplace. He was excited. He did not know quite what a play was, but he thought it must be something gay and splendid. He was happy to be going with his teacher and have a chance to see the Governor of Virginia himself up close.

But Ammonscossittee! What a dull-witted creature he was, uninterested in everything, too proud and arrogant to notice anything except how grand he was.

Perhaps he took no notice of a boy from Chota. Yet, of one thing Wayah was sure. Chota had sent one of her own to Virginia and Virginia was sealed to her. Only Chota would get the guns and the pots and the hatchets and blankets from the white men. Great Tellico would learn she could not take what rightfully belonged to the capital city of the Cherokees.

Surely, the white people must know that this was only fair, no matter what great things Ammonscossittee promised. Surely they would realize Chota's right.

If he, Wayah, had patience and long endurance and great courage, he would be the one to help Chota triumph, he would be the one to save his people. He could do it. He knew he could, for the Long Person still cradled him in its strength and the Ancient Red had not forgotten the child who had been given into its protection.

- 10 -

At the Theatre

ADAM stood on the steps of Brafferton Hall and waited for Master Dawson. He stood very still for he was wearing all his Sunday clothes and he felt very stiff and formal. But inside he was fidgeting mightily, full of impatience and excitement.

Overhead the November sky was bright with sunset. A few purplish dark clouds were knotted along the horizon and the black bare outlines of the maples swayed gently in the chilly wind.

People passed by on the Jamestown Road, some riding, some walking. Wayah expected each one to be the teacher, but each one went on by without a glance at the Indian boy in all his finery.

A chariot pulled by two horses came down the twilit street. The animals slowed and the carriage stopped. Adam looked at it curiously. Who could it be, halted there at the end of the walkway to the Brafferton?

Suddenly a head stuck out of the carriage and Master Dawson's voice called, "Hurry along, young Wolf."

Wayah gave a bounce of surprise and joy. He had expected to

walk, he hadn't known he would ride in one of the wheeled rooms. What a wonderful night this was beginning to be. He ran and Master Dawson reached down a hand to help him inside.

There was a woman in the carriage in a dress of deep blue, with her pale hair piled and heaped on her head. Wayah knew who this was, though he had never seen her before. This was Reverend Dawson's new wife.

They had been married in September. There had been no holiday or celebration, for the teacher was still in quiet mourning for his brother. In fact, William Squirrel had said that Mr. Stith, the College's new president, was angry with the Reverend Mr. Dawson for marrying at all.

Wayah thought that was why the master had not brought his wife to live in his apartments at Brafferton, but William Squirrel said no, none of the teachers was allowed to have his wife and family at the college, and that Mistress Dawson lived in a house of her own, in the town.

This had seemed strange to Wayah. What good did it do a man to be married if his wife lived somewhere far away from him, so that she could not fetch home the meat he killed and cook it for his meals? Now, however, looking at the bride he understood. With all those wide skirts and those pale curls, she would never be able to carry a deer haunch through the woods, to roast it over a hot fire. Perhaps she was sick or weak in some way.

Adam knew that actually Master Dawson never went hunting and that he ate at the college with the rest of them. But he had to stop and make himself think about these things. It had never seemed right and natural to him that the men of Williamsburg did not hunt and go to war, the way the men of Chota did.

Now Mistress Dawson spoke to him kindly. "I have heard of you often, Adam," she said. "I am very glad to make your acquaintance."

Adam smiled at her shyly. She might be unhealthy and not good for much, but she had gentle ways and he liked her. He felt that she was not a witch, either.

"All right, Sibby," called out the master and the driver spoke to the horses and slapped the reins. The carriage began to move.

"How now, Young Wolf," Dawson cried. "Did I not promise you

a ride? I have borrowed this carriage from a friend for the night. We will arrive in grand style for the play, like some rich planter or merchant."

Adam couldn't answer. He sat stiffly, but his eyes were alert, and it was all he could do to keep from waving his arms and shouting, as they turned onto Duke of Gloucester Street. Oh, even Otonee must believe this was a fine thing the white men had, this little room gliding along on wheels. He wished he could lean far out and see the fascinating wheels turning, turning.

In the dim light he saw the apothecary's shop where he and Duncan had bought sweets. And there was the candlemaker's place, yonder the tailor's. Wayah had been to town three times since June, all these places were familiar to him.

Once he had been shown the theatre, but it had seemed a plain building, lacking interest for him. He had not even comprehended what it was for. Now, approaching it, his eyes bulged out. What a marvel! He hadn't dreamed there were so many lanterns and candles in the whole of Virginia. It was as light as day! People milled about, horses and coaches and carriages thronged Waller Street before it, talk and laughter and the cries of hawkers filled the air.

The carriage stopped. Wayah jumped down and Master Dawson followed. He turned back to the vehicle and extended a hand to his wife and then stopped.

"Nay, here's a chance for Wolf to practice some manners," he said. "He shall hand my lady down. Assist Mistress Dawson, young Adam."

Wayah was puzzled. What was he supposed to hand this woman? She saw his bewilderment. "Give me your hand," she said. He held out his hand and she leaned on it while she sought for the step. Then she descended from the vehicle in a flurry of skirts and shawls.

"I was right," thought Adam. "She is too weak and sickly even to get out of the coach by herself." He felt sorry for Master Dawson.

Wayah looked about him. It was thrilling and a little frightening. Over there at the front of the theatre were the Indians from Great Tellico, dressed most beautifully in ornaments and clothes

of many colors. The white people pressed close around them and stared with great friendliness and curiosity. There were several white men with the Cherokees, grandly dressed men who must be officials of great importance. Adam felt certain one of them must be Governor Dinwiddie himself. Sure enough Master Dawson took his pupil up to the heavy-set, earnest-looking man and introduced him.

"Your Excellency, this is Adam Wolf, a Cherokee boy who has been with me all of Trinity Term. I brought him to the theatre to be with his compatriots," the teacher said.

The Governor inclined his head. "I am sure they will be glad to have him come into my box with them," he answered. "Has this boy made a good student?"

"Indeed, yes," the Reverend Mr. Dawson answered. "He has learned his catechism and writes a fair hand, but he has shown a greater talent for vulgar arithmetic."

The Governor looked pleased. He and Master Dawson and Watts began to talk about the problems of educating the Indians and how if there were more schooled Indians, disputes between red and white could be more satisfactorily settled.

Wayah turned his head to find Ammonscossittee staring at him insolently. The boy stared boldly back. He wished he could make everyone, Master Dawson and the Governor and all these admiring people realize just what a foolish dull-witted man this imposter was. But he couldn't, he knew. He did not have the words or the wit to make them understand.

The false Emperor began to speak to one of the braves. Wayah walked away from them. He would have nothing to do with them. They hated him and he despised them.

Moving through a rift in the crowd, he stood at the edge of a blazing circle of light. A man came skulking up out of the darkness. He was dirty and ragged and his eyes looked slyly here and there. When he saw Wayah, he stopped short.

"Well," he said softly, "a little Injun, for a fact. A prince, I doubt, by his clothes."

Wayah stood very still. He was afraid of the man. He wished for the hundredth time that Teacher Dawson would give him

back his tomahawk. If he had his hatchet, he wouldn't fear anybody.

The man moved closer. "Them's mighty pretty clothes now," he
whispered. "Fine as ever I seen. But here, now," he stooped and
touched the silver buckles on the boy's knees, "them things don't
go with a copper skin, not silver it don't. I'll just relieve you of
them and do you a mighty big favor and that's the mortal truth."

From somewhere he produced a little knife. Wayah started back
from the man but he reached out a dirty hand and held him fast.

"Be off!" someone cried and there was the sound of a blow. "Be
gone or I'll call the constable."

It was John Watts. The beggar slipped away into the darkness.
John Watts took Adam by the arm and led him back through the
crowd to the Governor, grumbling the while about thieves and
beggars who crowded the streets lately.

Now the party marched toward the theatre but stopped at the
entrance. There was a great scurrying and bowing around the Governor. Adam was shoved aside. He turned to look at the notice on
the wall beside him. He sounded out the syllables: "Traj—ee—dee
of Orr—tell—lo by Will—ee—am Shake—spear." What could it
mean?

They were ushered inside. The Governor and the false royal
couple went first. The interior was even brighter than outside,
with torches, candles, and lamps everywhere. Wayah stared at the
row of benches where the people were already seating themselves,
at the galleries like the ones in the church, and at the boxes along
the side walls. These boxes were very elegant with white and gold
paint and red curtains. Wayah was delighted to find that he was
going to sit in one.

The Governor and the Emperor and Empress and their child,
with John Watts, were to sit in the first of these. Adam would sit
with the Cherokee chiefs and white officials in another box, Watts
said. But when the boy turned to go, he found himself held fast.
The little prince from Great Tellico had tight hold of his breeches
and would not let go.

Governor Dinwiddie laughed. "A royal command, if I ever saw
one. Come with us, boy, and perhaps you can help John Watts in-

terpret, for by the same token, he's well-nigh talked his teeth out this day."

The audience turned to stare and point as the Cherokees took their places. Some even got up and sidled up to have a closer look. The Governor and the Empress and Emperor took seats at the front of the box. Dinwiddie, looking back at Wayah, moved his chair a little and John Watts squeezed the boy in.

"You can see better here," he told Adam.

Wayah felt this was very kind of both the white men, but he was not sure what he should be looking at. He felt certain that he must be intended to watch the platform at the front of the building. Yet, nothing was there to see but a big cloth and a flickering row of lights.

The little boy continued to stand by Wayah. He took a firm grip on his new found friend's sleeve with sticky, greasy fingers. Adam could see the dark smudges he made and he worried at what Master Dawson would say when he saw them.

The little boy held up something for Adam to see. It was a ribbon with a coil of brass wire on it. "Pretty," the boy said in Cherokee. "For you."

He gave it to Wayah and, dropping to his knees, crawled under the chairs to the rear of the box. He curled up against the wall and went to sleep. Adam turned back toward the pit below him. Hawkers went by selling broadsides and cakes and apples. The Governor bought cakes and apples for the Indians. Wayah found his round spicy cake delicious, but he hid the apple in his coat to take back to school with him.

Suddenly a man appeared on the platform. He made a long speech welcoming everyone. "Especially, I want to welcome tonight the Governor and his guests, the visiting Indian nobles," the man went on. "These Cherokees have come here to negotiate a treaty of peace and commerce with this Colony. I know I speak for all in wishing them a successful venture, a safe journey home, and prosperity thereafter. Now, for our play about Venice."

There was great applause. Some of the lights around the theatre were extinguished. The curtains opened. Before them was a painted picture of the street of some town. Wayah knew it wasn't

Williamsburg for the houses were different. Also the street was full of water and funny-looking boats.

Now men and women moved about talking too much and too fast. Adam could not understand what was taking place. Once he enjoyed it when a great many soldiers began to dash about and fight with swords and knives. He was stirred to the marrow, but not as much as the Empress who jumped from her seat and pleaded with the men to stop the battle before they were all hurt.

The curtains closed and there was some white man's music of high quavering squeaks and low trembling grumbles. Wayah wished they would stop. It hurt his ears. The Emperor talked loudly to Governor Dinwiddie about the people from Chota, how they were upstarts and unimportant men among the Cherokees and were not to be trusted.

Wayah was tight with anger, hearing this. He longed to say it was not so. He half-rose from his chair to tell the Governor or John Watts that the warriors of Chota were the true elders, leaders of wisdom and authority. It didn't seem possible that the crooked words of Ammonscossittee would be believed.

Still, he did not speak. It was not that he was afraid, but simply that he didn't know how to put his thoughts into English words. Perhaps John Watts could tell the Governor the truth. Should he ask the translator to do this? He sat down slowly to think this over.

The music stopped, the curtains opened once again. The actors began to speak. And so the night passed as the curtains opened and closed, opened and closed. Wayah yawned often and at last rested his head on the railing of the box, for just a moment. . . .

"No-vem-ber. De-cem-ber," Adam said the words over to himself. They were pretty words, though cold. They sounded the way the day looked, he thought, lifting his head up to stare out the window at the cold blue sky, the bare trees tipped with sparkling ice. A fire roared on the hearth in the schoolroom and it was warm in there, though not so warm as it would be in his grandfather's winter hot house in Chota. But he did not mind the cold. He was used to weather, hot or cold, wet or dry.

He was tough. He would survive anything. He knew this was

so. Had he not already defeated Ammonscossittee, the false Emperor of the Cherokees? Was he not still the only Cherokee boy at Brafferton? And did that not mean that Chota was still favored above other Cherokee towns?

After the people from Great Tellico returned to their homes, he had been sure a great many boys would be sent to the school. He had waited for their arrival for days. But no one had come. It must be that the white people had realized that Ammonscossittee was a pretender. Probably they knew now that they must do business with Chota alone.

"Have you finished your sums, Wolf?" asked Master Dawson. "Then write out your multiplication table in a fair hand. Do not be idle. Christmas holidays are very close now, we mustn't wait."

Christmas, and after that New Year's Day, these were important days to the white men. They meant that the year had rolled as deep into winter as it would roll. The days were short now, the boys crossed the college yard to the chapel at the hour called seven rather than the one called six, because of the brevity of daylight. As they walked back and forth under the naked trees, their breath made feathery plumes in the frosty air.

Soon, soon, it would be spring and the warm days would come, and the corn stand tall in its beautiful green leaves. Then it would begin to tassel and Two Sticks would come to Williamsburg to fetch home Wayah, a boy of the Real People.

His quill had grown dull. He stood up to take it to the Master's desk to be sharpened, but suddenly he was dizzy, his head circled and swam, and he had to sit down. He looked around hoping no one had noticed. It would never do to show a sign of weakness. But several times lately he had been overtaken by dizziness. He wished he could ask Otonee what caused it.

When he awoke next morning, he was cold under his blanket. The big attic room was heated only by the warmth of the chimneys that rose up through it on the way to the roof. Yet Wayah had never noticed its being cold before. He shivered and he could not stop. He shivered all the way to the chapel. Even in the building, which seemed so warm his head felt tight and hot, he shivered and shivered and shivered. What was happening to him?

- II -

Fever Dreams

WAYAH held in his hand his winking red stone, the magic stone which had protected him for so long. While he watched, the fires within it dimmed. It grew dull and somber. Fearfully he closed his fingers over it.

"My stone is dying!" he wailed aloud. "It cries for blood. It must have blood to save its life."

He had brought it here to this cave in the Cherokee Mountains where it would be safe, where its magic strength would work against the enemies of Wayah, the Wolf. But he had waited too late to find it this hiding place. All its vivid sparkling soul was flowing from it.

He laid it on the damp sand of the cave floor. Its blood cried out for a sacrifice of blood. Quickly he poured the little pot of warm deer's blood over it. Had he waited too late to try to save it? Was the stone too weak to drink? Would it never again be a mighty amulet working to help a boy of the Real People?

The blood sank down, down, down into the stone till once more it was alive. It gleamed and flashed, its terrible power stirred within it once more. It lived.

Wayah sighed with relief. When he had drained the last of the blood from the pot, he wrapped the stone in a piece of soft doeskin and laid it on a shelf of rock. Here it would be safe. In the cool darkness of the cave no one would ever see it who was not fit to gaze upon its might. Here with the passing days it would grow stronger and stronger.

Wayah turned and made his way along the wall toward the front of the cave. But something blocked the entrance, a great huge-shouldered beast with wide-open, slavering, savagely snarling jaws! He was trapped.

The bear stood up on its hind legs and walked into the cave. Wayah backed away. His tomahawk was gripped tightly in his hand. The beast sank to all fours suddenly and its angry little eyes shone. It shambled closer and closer, its head swinging back and forth before the boy, back and forth.

Wayah gave way slowly, keeping out of reach of those great knobby paws and snapping fangs. A step back, another, and then his shoulders came hard up against the cave wall. A quick glance around told him there wasn't even a crevice for him to slip into. The cave ended here. He had no choice but to fight the bear.

The bear stood up again. It spread its vast arms and the light gleamed dully along its claws. Wayah had never imagined that there was such a huge bear in the whole wide land. He crouched and the bear lunged, grabbing at him with its giant paws. Wayah ducked and slashed out with his tomahawk. The bear screamed and staggered back with its forearm dripping blood.

For a moment it paused, surprised. Then roaring, it towered over him, tremendous and overwhelming, a storm of claws and teeth and iron muscles. He hacked at it again and again with his tomahawk. He could feel the blade slice into the bear's body, he could see the blood, but the bear seemed not to feel the blows.

With a sudden slap it knocked the tomahawk away and swept Wayah into its arms. Its paws pulled him up to its furry chest and strained him against its great hot body, tighter and tighter. Wayah struggled to draw his knife. It was a white man's knife with a

steel blade, as sharp and terrible as a rattlesnake's tooth, and a handle just right for his small hand.

He could feel the handle. His fingers were on it, yet he could not draw it. The bear squeezed him harder and harder. His chest was bursting, his face crushed deeper into that thick hair. He struggled for breath, fighting against the iron bonds that closed around him.

Someone was crying and sobbing and gasping, but Wayah could not believe it was himself. He did not think there was room in his lungs for anything at all, he was dying.

It seemed days to Wayah that he stayed there in the bear's horrible embrace. The ache of his bursting chest spread to his head and throbbed till it seemed he must split open and die in little pieces. The bear's grip tightened and tightened.

All at once the knife was in Wayah's hand. With the touch of it his strength returned. He freed his arm and stabbed the bear in the chest and belly, over and over, ripping and tearing at the flesh until it hung in bloody shreds.

The bear bent its head and sank its teeth into the boy's arm. Warm blood spurted out in a red arc. He cried out at the pain and tried to jerk his arm away.

Master Dawson's voice warned him. "No, no, Wolf, lie quietly. The surgeon will soon be done."

Where was the bear? Here was a white man cutting at his arm, as he lay in the infirmary, covered with blankets. A low fire burned on the hearth. But where was the bear? He couldn't see it anywhere. He had killed the beast, he remembered. Now he must sing a song to the White Bear, leader of all the bears and blood kin to the Real People. He must cover the slain bear's body with leaves, and all its spilled blood too, so that it would rise again.

He got an armful of leaves and scattered them over the still form on the cave floor, singing the bear song all the while. At last he had pacified the bear's spirit. As he left the cave, he glanced back. The new bear heaved up out of the pile of leaves, taller and taller. Its eyes glinted red and cruel. With a roar it rushed at Wayah. The boy spun around to fight once again and found himself facing Grigley.

He flinched. He did not want to kill Grigley, much as he hated him. It was not right. Yet, the white boy came at Wayah, raking at him with claws. Wayah had no choice. He plunged the knife at Grigley's white face, but he couldn't seem to reach it. At each slash Grigley floated away, backward, receding, his white face growing smaller and smaller in the black corners of the cave, until. . . .

When Wayah woke the second time, he was alone. He hurt all over, especially his head and chest. He tried to lift the arm the bear had bitten but it was too much effort. Suddenly the door opened and Mrs. Dawson came slipping into the room. When she saw him, she looked pleased.

"Adam Wolf, you're really awake at last!" she cried. She laid a cool hand on his forehead. "Yes, the fever's lessened. I must fetch you something to drink. Now, lie quietly till I come back."

Adam did what the gentle lady told him. There was little else he could do. Mistress Dawson brought back a bowl of something evil smelling. She lifted his head and made him swallow a spoonful. It tasted awful and made his stomach churn. He turned his head aside a little.

"Swallow just a bit more, it's only wine-whey," she coaxed. And because she was so kind and her hands so gentle, he swallowed another spoonful.

She wiped his forehead with a damp cloth and rearranged his blankets. He drifted off into dreams once again. Suddenly his eyes were open and there stood Master Dawson and the surgeon. The surgeon shook his head.

"I've bled him to draw the sanguinary humors from his body, and I've given him calomel and I've physicked him with many herbs," the surgeon said. "All those things should have had him well mended before this. But Indians—perhaps they don't respond to our medicines the way white people do. I've never treated Indians except these boys at the school."

They went out of the room and Wayah lay listening to the sound of his own shallow breathing. He was going to die. Everything he had done was in vain. He was not going to be able to get the trade for Chota. No one was going to know how he had suffered and endured. He was never going to see his home again. He wished he could hold his red stone in his hand one last time.

Every time Wayah woke up, he expected to find himself dying. It was so hard to breathe and his head was always floating off near the ceiling. The fever dreams scared him and the hours when he was awake were even more wretched. At nights, the dark stretched before him so endlessly it seemed years till daylight lit the windows. If he had not been too weak and light-headed, he would have tried to go after his red magic crystal.

He repeated all the prayers he knew to the Ancient Red and to the Long Person. He said over and over the catechism which Master Dawson had made him learn. He called for help from the white man's God. Yet, it seemed to him that he could not live much longer.

His breath came and went so quickly and every time it went it was harder to whistle it back into his chest. He turned and turned in his bed, restlessly. Once, as he turned, he thought he saw the door opening. But in his fever he saw the door open often and people and animals and Otonee and everyone he had ever known come through. So, this time he paid no attention until he saw Duncan's red hair. When Duncan came close, he saw suddenly that the white boy was real. It was no dream.

"Adam Wolf," whispered the other boy. "Are you better? I can't stay but a spell. Master don't want us up here with you. But I thought mayhap there was something I could do for you. You know, something you might not want to ask Master."

Wayah stared at the white boy.

Duncan smiled. "Your eyes have got as big as buckets," he commented. "You look like my dog at home when he fell in a sink hole and it was two weeks till we found him."

"I will die," announced Wayah and he looked at the curtained windows. He passed his hot dry hands over his face. He wished he could tell Duncan about his magic stone. After he was dead Duncan could use it. But he knew it was not possible. Once a stranger gazed on the stone, or touched it, it would lose its power.

It was dreadful to die all alone in a strange land. The whites would treat his body as they wished. They would waste no time in scalping him. They would take his scalp to one of the shops in the town and his spirit would wander forever, restless and unhappy. The white men would not care. What was an Indian boy to them?

He watched the fire shadows on the ceiling. If his scalp was sent back to Chota for decent burial, all would be well. Duncan would do this thing for him. He must. They were friends.

He struggled for words. "I will die," he began. "White men will take my scalp. No, no. Must send scalp to Chota. Duncan, this you do. Take scalp, send to Chota. Do not let scalp of Wayah the Wolf stay in Williamsburg."

Duncan was horrified. "White men don't take scalps," he exclaimed. "At least folks in Williamsburg don't. Nobody wants your scalp."

"Here in town," Wayah insisted. "Many scalps in many shops. For sale. I saw."

Duncan looked puzzled. Then he grinned. "You mean the wig shops?" he asked. "Those aren't scalps there. Those are wigs—you know, false hair for people who don't like to fool with keeping their hair long and curled. They buy the false hair to wear when they dress up.

Wayah wondered if this was true. Yes, he decided, Duncan wouldn't lie to him. He was greatly relieved.

Suddenly Duncan began to laugh. "Wonder what folks would say if Governor Dinwiddie went to church wearing a red Injun's scalp instead of a powdered periwig?" he asked. "Hey, Wolf, no wonder you've got the collywobbles, lying here thinking such mournful things. You ain't going to die. Think about Easter Vacation. I aim to take you home with me, if Master's willing."

Adam smiled a little.

"See, you're beginning to mend already," cried Duncan. "I'll wager you'll be out of this sickbed in a week."

Perhaps he was right. Certainly when he was gone, Wayah felt calmer and much better. When the housekeeper brought his broth and his vile-tasting tea, they went down his throat more easily than they ever had before.

In the night he was sick and scared again, but toward morning his fever broke and he drifted into a deep and peaceful sleep.

When next the housekeeper and the master came to see him, they agreed that he was recovering.

A few evenings later William Squirrel and Gideon Green Peach came to visit him. William Squirrel looked at him earnestly. "Master says you will soon be up," he announced. "That is good. Now I and the fool warrior are the only Indians. The two Pamunkey boys have been sent home."

"They die," declared Gideon. "They go home to die."

William Squirrel laughed scornfully. "The Saponi knows, as he knows all things," he said.

"I cure," cried Gideon. "I cure you. I cure Pamunkeys."

He rushed up beside the bed. "I scratch you with comb of rattlesnake teeth," he explained. "Scatch all over. Let evil out."

He then leaped to the middle of the room. "I dance," he told them.

Away he went this way and that, flinging his legs about madly, and clapping his hands against his sides. Then he came back to the bed and with many gulping noises pretended to suck the evil from Wayah's sick body, spitting it out of his mouth to the floor.

Wayah had seen the conjurors at Chota suck worms, stones, various bits of cloth and sticks from ailing people and cure them. He wished Master Dawson had let Gideon minister to him. He felt sure he would have recovered much sooner. Certainly it would have been better than being stuck with a lancet and bled time after time or being made to drink all those dreadful bitter medicines.

However the white man's medicines must have helped for a few days later he was up. His head felt queer and his legs shook under him, but he could get around. Every day he grew a little stronger, though there were times when the fever came back and nights when he was shaken with pain. Some days he had to lie alone in his attic room, too sick to go to school.

At such times Duncan came up to talk to him of his home, a plantation some miles away from Williamsburg, and of Adam's visit there with him during the holidays. Duncan longed for his own home, just as Wayah did.

Now Wayah felt he and the white boy were once again the best of friends. He was glad. He could not be friends with Gideon Green Peach. He understood Gideon's ways well enough, since they were the ways of his own home and of his own people, but Gideon lived in a ghost world. It made Wayah a little fearful to watch him. He was like a boy in delirium, the things he saw and spoke of were never real.

As for William Squirrel, Wayah had no use for him either. He sometimes felt sorry for the one-handed boy and once he wondered if the Shawnee had cut off his own hand hoping to cut away his own Indian ways. William Squirrel yearned desperately to be a white boy. Wayah could see that strong desire always waiting deep at the bottom of his eyes.

Yet, the Shawnee was still proud. He never tried to be friends with the white boys. He stood aloof. But always and ever he did what Master Dawson said to do, and told the other Indians to obey. He prodded Wayah and Gideon to drop their Indian ways and be as he was. Wayah despised him for it.

No, Duncan was the one with whom he could be happy and easy. Adam was anxious for the holidays too, to see the great house where Duncan lived, to learn to shoot a gun and drive a carriage and all the other things Duncan had promised to teach him.

The winter was long and hard. There were many illnesses in the school. Even Master Dawson himself had to take to his bed, while a master from the college came to teach them, a man who seemed always to be thinking about something else. He could not remember their names and tried to make Gideon do Grigley's Latin and gave Grigley the beating he had promised Duncan, which pleased everyone but Grigley.

February went by and suddenly the maples were blossoming. The sky was blue. In the mornings no ice floated on the surface of the water in the fire buckets. It was spring at last. Wayah, coming from chapel, lifted his face to the warm morning sun and prayed to the Ancient Red, "Take me home, take me home."

There was still such a long while before Two Sticks came for him he did not know how he could bear it. Hilary Term ended finally and the April holidays began.

"You are to go with me," Duncan told Adam. "My father wrote Master. The carriage comes for us at noon, so be ready."

Wayah didn't know what to do. He didn't know how to go on a

visit. Master Dawson took him upstairs and helped him put his clothes in his trunk and strap it up to take away with him.

"It will do you good to go," the teacher said. "You need a change of air and better food than we can give you here. But mind you, behave as a scholar of Brafferton Hall should."

Adam nodded, trying to hold his excitement inside himself.

He and Duncan waited together for the coach. Some men were repairing one of the walls of an outbuilding, replacing some bricks that had crumbled during the hard freezes of winter. Adam reflected that somehow he had never had the chance to see the curious red stones made and he was just about to ask Duncan if he knew where it was done, when the coach came in sight.

The two boys climbed in, and one thing Adam did not think of for two weeks was bricks.

- 12 -

"Adam Wolf Done It!"

ADAM was unstrapping his chest when he heard the other two Indian boys climbing the stairs to the Brafferton attic after supper. He took out his coat and hung it on a peg without looking around. He could feel the eyes of William Squirrel and Gideon Green Peach on him. But he said nothing. Instead he went back to his trunk and picked up a shirt. Carefully he shook out the wrinkles and then hung it on the wall beside his coat.

Finally William Squirrel burst out. "What was it like? How is it in the house of a white person?"

There was deep envy in the Shawnee's voice. It exasperated Adam. He didn't want William Squirrel to envy him. And he didn't care to talk to him about his visit to Duncan's plantation.

Slowly Wayah turned around. The Shawnee sat waiting eagerly. Wayah shrugged. "It was good," he grunted. "Big house, very fine."

The house was bigger than Brafferton Hall, much bigger, with many slaves to sweep the thick colorful carpets, to keep the clothes tidy and the beds with their white, white linen sheets in order, and to look after Duncan's five redheaded brothers and sisters.

"House for cows, house for pigs, for chickens, house for cooking, house for water, and one for dead meat," Adam went on. "All beds made of feathers. Very soft. Too many things to eat. Strange foods such as not here at school."

He could still make his breath catch in his throat at the thought of the big dining room table, laden with food. Always two or three kinds of meat, as well as fish and wild fowls and sometimes piles of smooth white bread made of wheat instead of corn. And wonderful sweet things called pies and cakes, which Duncan and Wayah ate all the time. Duncan drank much milk but it was tasteless stuff to Adam, so Mistress Duncan gave him hot chocolate or tea with many spoons of sugar in it.

He struggled to tell this to the one-armed boy, but it was hard to find the words. Nor was it any easier to tell the Shawnee about Duncan's mother who was so tiny and gentle and who worried so because Adam's ribs stuck out and circles lay under his eyes. Or about Colonel Duncan, who was so big and powerful and rich and owned so many fine things, yet who could play ball with the children or wade in the streams after minnows and laugh and have gay times like a boy.

Colonel Duncan had shown Wayah a bow which he had bought from a Mattapony chieftain once. He asked to be shown how to shoot it. Wayah strung the bow and made the arrows and he and Colonel Duncan and Duncan took turns shooting at a target. Colonel Duncan praised Wayah's shooting, but he and his son found it too hard, so instead they practiced with a musket. Wayah had never shot a gun before. He was fascinated with the weapon and made up his mind to have one of his own. Otonee would not approve, he knew, but then there were many things his grandfather did not understand.

There had been pony rides and rides on the "wild mare," a plank loosely fastened to a stump. Wayah and one of the younger brothers sat on one end and Duncan and his youngest sister on the other. They had spun round and round and up and down till they were dizzy and ready to fall off with laughter.

Duncan's mother had played the spinet for them, sitting in front of a black box, not at all afraid of its huge row of fiercely grinning white teeth. By stroking the teeth gently she made the box sing and she sang with it. Adam listened politely and thanked her, but he did not like it. He would never grow used to the white man's music.

"How many white men?" asked Gideon suddenly, whirling around from where he stood at the window. "How many you kill? All sleeping at night. Indian not locked up, not tied. Many knives. Take knives, kill white people sleeping in bed. Kill all whites!"

William Squirrel lashed out at him angrily. "Why should he kill them? They are his friends. He has been a guest in their house. You are a fool!" He lit the candle and began to read his book.

Adam finished his unpacking with a troubled heart. Gideon went down his ladder and out into the night. Frogs creaked and purred from every ditch and a whippoorwill called, like an unhappy spirit.

What William Squirrel had said was true. The Duncans had been kind to him, they had been his friends. So much so that he had hated to leave, had dreaded coming back here to the cold bare school and the same unvarying meals and the continual effort to master the tasks set him.

Yet, he was an Indian boy. This he knew more than ever now. Even the Duncans had not been able to forget it or to make him forget it. They had not stared at him curiously or treated him as a stranger. Still, while he was there with them, he had never been closer to his home. He was a part of the life of Chota and had a place there that he would never be able to find among the whites no matter how long he searched. He was proud to be one of the Real People and the strength and goodness of his race beat strongly in him.

Why should he think so highly of the things Duncan had? He, himself, had a very fine home in the midst of beautiful mountains. His father was a great warrior and teller of tales. His mother was gentle and kind, she could weave cloth in bright designs and tan hides until they were as soft as goose down. At home there were always good things to eat too, barbecued pumpkin, potato and persimmon breads to dip in sweet bear's oil, and choice pieces of any game the forests offered, or fish or birds, or a variety of nuts and fruits, for that matter.

Was he growing to be like William Squirrel? Was he going to become in the end the kind of worthless lightning-split tree Otonee had predicted? He climbed into bed and lay staring up at the sloping attic ceiling.

Was there no choice? Did the white men always kill Indians, one way or another? For William Squirrel was dead, his eyes and heart were empty of anything but envy of the white men. And Gideon Green Peach was dead, he had nothing inside himself but foolish dreams of revenge and hate.

He *would* survive. He had to. Somehow he would live through till the time when Two Sticks came for him. It was not long now. His glowing red stone would protect him and keep him safe.

He turned on his side and went at once to sleep.

The bell rang. The Indian boys arose and dressed and waited for Master Dawson to unlock the door at the foot of the steps. They marched across the yard where the robins and thrushes stopped caroling long enough to watch them. In the chapel the white boys were already seated. Duncan turned and gave Wayah a grin over his shoulder.

Wayah, sinking to his knees, thought that though the white man had many good and wonderful things, he paid for them dearly. What, in all the land, was worth losing one's freedom, to be ordered about by clocks and bells, to spend so much of one's time cased up in stiff clothes and pinching shoes? Even at the Duncan plantation, bells had rung and meals had to be eaten at set hours and children were bundled off to bed, sleepy or not.

Master Dawson had not spoken to Adam since his return. He wanted to be able to tell the master that he had behaved well on his visit, that he had done as he was told. Also that the vacation had been good for him. Once more he felt strong and well. The fever had not touched him once while he was at the plantation.

This morning Master Dawson did not look at the boys. He conducted the service with a grave face and his eyes cast down. There was an air of unpleasant anticipation and of worry seeping through

the school. Wayah noticed it as soon as he stepped inside the college door and it made him uneasy.

The Brafferton scholars marched back to their schoolroom. Master Dawson did not follow them in. Instead he went to his apartments. The boys waited in silence a moment or two, then they began to whisper and poke one another. Grigley beat one of the smaller boys with his knotted handkerchief. Two of the others tossed a book back and forth.

Suddenly Master Dawson entered the room. The boys hastily took their places and opened their books. Behind the teacher came one of the teachers of the college and President Stith. All the men looked stern and Master Dawson looked sorrowful. He frowned at Grigley and the boys who had been throwing the book, but he did not say anything. Instead President Stith went to Dawson's great desk and stood beside it.

"Young gentlemen," he began severely, "a very serious offense has occurred at our college. Some one or another of the scholars is guilty of a crime. There is no other word for it. But let not the sinner be deceived, nor any other of you. The truth will always out. The eye of God is ever upon you. Whatever sin or abomination you commit, He sees and He will not let it lie buried."

He looked around the room and then continued, "Last year our well-beloved President Dawson lost the setting from his ring. A great garnet, both beautiful and valuable. It was believed that the stone had fallen from the ring and would be found in the college yard. A reward was offered. But no one came forward. Our President died still grieving for his property, a keepsake from his own father, a handsome piece of jewelry."

He pointed an accusing finger at them and thundered, "Now it occurs to me that perhaps the stone was *pried* from the ring and deliberately stolen. For it has been found, and in a place where it could never have got except by some human agency. Whether the stone was pried loose or not, by the same token, concealing it was as wicked as pilfering it. It was a crime and a sin and a scandal."

Whatever can he be talking about, Wayah worried.

"Now," went on President Stith, "let him who stole the stone come forward and admit his guilt. Do not augment one sin by adding to it the sin of lying. Confession is good. It can help cleanse the soul. Let no boy doubt that the Almighty knows what he has done. Now let him publicly admit his guilt to hasten that time when he can earn forgiveness for this base deed."

It was a bad thing, Adam decided. Whatever it was, it was a bad thing.

The students stirred uneasily. President Stith stood grim and silent. Gradually the sun-filled room became quiet. Wayah looked around. All the boys, even Duncan, were staring at the table where the three Indians sat.

"They think one of us did this thing!" thought Wayah in surprise. "How could I do it when I don't even know what it is?"

The moments grew longer and longer. Still no one spoke, still the eyes of the white boys never shifted from the Indians. Grigley's lips moved and voicelessly he spoke the words, "Adam Wolf done it."

Suddenly William Squirrel stood up at his place. "I am the one," he said quietly. "I put the red stone in its hiding place."

The red stone in its hiding place! Wayah was startled. They might easily be talking about his magic crystal.

Master Dawson gave a deep groan. "Oh, William Squirrel!" he cried sorrowfully. "Not you. Not you. You have been with us over three years. You have been baptised. Why would you want to steal my brother's garnet?"

The Shawnee hung his head. He said nothing. The master approached the Indian boys' desk, holding out his open hand. The garnet lay in it. "For this, a vain bauble, you would risk your immortal soul? You would forget all my trouble and kindness to you?"

Wayah gasped and stood up. He trembled all over. "My stone!" he cried out in Cherokee. "Give me back my magic stone!" He flung himself at Master Dawson.

The teacher staggered and seized the boy by the arm. "What is the meaning of this?" he shouted. "Sirrah, what are you doing?"

Wayah drew back and stared at the master. He searched frantically for the English words. "It is mine. Stone has great strongness," he whispered. "It stayed safe in wall. I stayed safe. It helps me. It is my stone."

President Stith took a step toward him with his face threatening. But Master Dawson held up his hand. "Adam Wolf, do you mean that you put the stone in the wall? You, not William Squirrel?"

"My stone," repeated Wayah numbly and not till Master shook him gently did he look up. "Did you put this stone behind the brick in the wall of that outhouse yonder?" the teacher asked quietly.

"Wayah nodded. "It was give to me. River and Fire give it to me."

Master Dawson stared down at his pupil. "Where were you when they gave it to you?" he asked. "How did they give it to you?"

Adam nodded out the window. "There, by walkway. In the grass. They put it in my hand. My stone," he said faintly.

Thomas Dawson looked at President Stith. "It has been a misunderstanding," he said at last. "The boy must have found the stone where it dropped from the ring. He thought it was an amulet or something sent to protect him from us. Perhaps he was right. Perhaps he needed help."

He paused and shook his head sadly. "And I failed him."

"Humph," said the President. "Let us hope you have not let your Christian charity blind you to any wrongdoing." Then he spoke to the Shawnee. "You, there, Squirrel, or whatever your name is. How came you to confess falsely to this crime? How came you to show such ingratitude?"

William Squirrel stood a moment longer with bent head. Suddenly he raised his eyes and met Master Dawson's gaze. "Sir," he said slowly. "I said that I took the stone because I could see that all of these"—he swept his hand around the room—"all thought an Indian boy had taken it. 'Now,' I told myself, 'they think all Indians are thieves and liars. If I say I took the stone, perhaps they will think all Indian boys thieves, but not liars.' So I said it."

He looked down once more, adding, "Besides, it is my fault."

"What do you mean?" inquired Master Dawson.

"Sir," said the Shawnee. "I knew Adam Wolf did not understand. He did not know that garnets are red stones. He did not understand what had been lost. I knew that he had something hidden outside. I thought perhaps it was the garnet, but I said nothing. I hoped perhaps he would be discovered with it and that you would be vexed with him, Master. I did not want him to be the Indian student who pleased you best."

Wayah listened, straining to understand. Was the stone really not his? Had this beautiful fiery crystal belonged all the time to the white men? Certainly it belonged to them now. Master Dawson's long pale hand closed over it tightly.

Wayah was sure he would never see its lovely flames again. Two Sticks had better come for him quickly, for now he had no protection. Nothing now could keep him from splitting in two. Nothing could save him but going back to Chota soon.

Master Dawson turned to the President. "Lay not up for yourself treasures on earth," he said sadly. "Sir, I think this incident is closed. I hope that none of us will have reason to remember it ever again. Tell the College that what was lost has been found, that I am grateful to all who searched. And the reward shall go to the workman who found the garnet behind the loose brick."

Wayah sank back into his place with his head in his hands. He did not know whom or what to call upon for help. How many days until the corn tasseled and Two Sticks came to Williamsburg? Could he stay alive till then? Oh, how could he hurry that time up?

- 13 -

Two Sticks Returns

THE Second Commandment," wrote Adam slowly, "is that thou shalt not make to thyself any graven image."

He had written this many times in the past weeks. Master Dawson had given him the sentence to copy, to improve his penmanship. Adam was not deceived. He knew the teacher expected him to learn something from these words. He did not understand how he could learn from them. He did not know what they meant.

He looked out the window at the college garden, growing behind the main building. He could see half a row of light green corn, waist high almost.

"Grow, grow," he whispered fiercely.

Master Dawson seemed to think the red stone was a graven image. Perhaps graven meant "buried." The stone had been buried. But it was not an image. It was a magic crystal, deep and full of fire, moving and shining with its own power.

Only it was not a magic stone. It was merely a white man's ornament. It was nothing and it had no power.

All the time he had been at Brafferton then, he had been alone.

Fire and Water had not been there to help him as he had supposed. He had had no defenses, no one had cared for him or protected him. The thought frightened him.

He trembled a little. He must have been split into a thousand pieces without knowing it. Panic seized him and he almost sprang up and ran.

No, no, it was not so. He *knew* it was not so. He had managed somehow to stay whole. A Cherokee boy did not surrender easily, and he had not surrendered. Though he had stood alone and unaided and almost friendless, he was still upright and strong and not split. He had not, in truth, needed the stone. All the courage and long endurance of the Real People had held him together. The lightning had struck, but it had not torn him in two. He had suffered but he had not split. He set his jaws. He had not and he *would* not.

"Wolf," Master Dawson spoke.

Wayah turned to his work and began again, "The Second Commandment."

Yesterday at noon break he had gone into the garden to look at the corn. The gardner had found him and pulled him out by an ear. "You ain't going to trample my corn and beans, you little savage," he roared. "You git, and don't you let me catch you putting your thieving hands on nothing around here."

Rubbing his ear Adam had made his way back to Brafferton Hall and sat on the steps, alone. When Duncan came up to him, he turned away. He was afraid of Duncan and his blazing hair and his blue eyes, now that he no longer had his protective amulet. Besides, the white boys had laughed at him for hiding the stone. Perhaps Duncan was laughing too. He did not want to have anything to do with any of them.

He didn't want to have anything to do with William Squirrel either, although he and the Shawnee boy were alone in the attic room now. Gideon Green Peach had gone down the rope one night and failed to return, gone off to run with the wolves, Squirrel said.

Oh, how Wayah had longed to follow, to be free of Brafferton Hall forever. But he had to stay. He knew it. It could not be much longer now. Surely he could live these next few weeks.

". . . any graven image."

He made a round black spot at the end of the sentence. Then the bell rang for the break. He didn't really want to go outside with the others. Yet he wanted a closer look at that corn. How much longer before it began to tassel?

"Adam," someone spoke to him.

Wayah looked around. There was Duncan grinning at him. "Don't be such a hedgehog," said the white boy. "Every time I come near you, you curl up and stick out your prickles. Why can't we be friends any more?"

Wayah stared at him solemnly.

"Ain't we friends?" Duncan asked. "We've not got much time left to be friends in, if you're leaving soon. We had a heap of good times together, Adam. When you go away, I'd like to be your friend still and hope you might come to my house again some day."

Slowly Adam smiled. He would be foolish to forget a friendship, no matter what had happened. Duncan *was* his friend. They need not fear each other.

"We friends," he replied.

"Listen, Adam, tomorrow's a half holiday," Duncan went on. "Come to town with me. We can go swimming at the mill pond first. And then see what's doing in the town."

"I go with you," promised Adam. And he went.

The May afternoon was bright and warm. Wayah felt better than he had for a long time, walking along the street at the side of his friend.

But Duncan was frowning. "I can't stay the afternoon," he told Wayah sorrowfully. "I'm leaving Williamsburg to go back to the plantation this very afternoon. My father's going away to London on business, and he wants me home till he comes back."

He laughed aloud suddenly. "I'll be running the plantation all by myself, except for Mama and the overseer and three or four house servants. Anyway, we've time for walking around a little and buying some sweets—handfuls. Papa gave me some money."

He grinned gleefully and led the way past the sign of the Unicorn and into the apothecary's. The proprietor smiled at them.

"You two be mighty friendly for such different chaps," he said. "I've heard tell that birds of a feather flock together, but you couldn't hope to see such different feathers as yours." He pointed at the red head and then at Adam's.

Duncan answered readily, "Red hair or black hair, macaroons taste good to both, Apothecary. Let us have a dozen."

They walked out and down the street past the church, too busy eating to do any talking. They crossed the great green that led up to the Governor's Palace. Beyond was a gunsmith's shop and Adam paused to gaze longingly at the display of guns.

"Come on, come on," urged Duncan, tugging at Adam's sleeve. "You don't need a gun, the way you can shoot a bow and arrow."

They ran across the Market Square, scaring up four flickers. Up the street Duncan walked along the top of the hitching rail in front of a house. He urged the Indian boy to try but Adam wouldn't. There were too many people around to watch him. He was stared at enough, just walking along.

"Now, it's follow the leader, Adam, and you have to do this with me," shouted the redhead.

Away he dashed, Wayah at his heels, up some steps that arched before a white door. He banged the knocker and whipped away quickly down the steps on the opposite side. He stopped at the corner of Colonial Street to look back and laugh at the servant who had answered the knock.

Duncan grinned mischievously. "It's my duty to torment the townfolks all I can," he explained to Wayah, who grinned back.

At the printing office Adam gazed in the open door to hear a great clattering and clanging. Duncan pointed to the books and pamphlets on display in the window. "That's too much like school. Books, ugh! Quick, let's away!"

They passed under three iron sugar loafs which Duncan said was the sign of a grocer. "Smell the coffee," he cried and sniffed deeply. Then he pointed. "Look yonder. There's where they sell scalps."

Adam followed him across the street. It was a wigmaker's shop and there stood many wigs, all powdered and curled on their wooden stands.

"Foolish white men," Wayah commented. "Put clothes on back, on feet, even on hair!"

"Maybe I ought to sell them all this hair," Duncan said, pulling

Wayah's queue. "We could take the money and buy some more sweets."

"Redhead scalp worth more," laughed Wayah and he grabbed Duncan's hair with one hand and circled around it with an imaginary scalping knife.

They chased each other toward an intersection. "This is Botetourt Street," Duncan said. "My aunt lives down there. That's my father's traveling chariot waiting in front of the house and that means he's through with his shopping and has come for me. So, I must go."

Duncan glanced back to the Indian boy. "My father brought something today for me to give you. I hope you like it."

He took Wayah's hand and pressed something into it. He closed the Cherokee's fingers around it.

"Now, you have been nearly a year at the school and all those months the clock has ordered you about," Duncan said. "I've heard you complain about it. So my father and I thought we'd give you a watch. With your own watch you can order time about to suit yourself. Look and see."

Adam stared down at the round silver watch with its white face, slender hands and twelve numerals. He'd seen watches before. He rubbed his fingers over the cold smooth surface. What an awesome thing, to own a watch, a thing that surely had a sort of life of its own, that moved and spoke with a little chirping voice.

Duncan gave him a tiny key and showed him how to wind it and to move the hands about on the face of the timepiece. "See, you don't have to wait till noon for it to be time to eat," he pointed out. "When you're hungry, you can move the hands up to twelve and eat right away. And if you *really* want to get the best of time, just let the watch run down and forget it."

The boys smiled at each other. Wayah knew Duncan was only joking. Yet he was touched that the Duncans had given him something. And a watch was certainly an excellent gift. Nobody in Chota had a watch.

"I will not let little voice stop," Wayah said softly. "I will make it go every day. It will say to me Dun-can, Dun-can. I will think of you."

"And I'll think of you," Duncan promised. "Come back to Williamsburg some day, Adam, and come and see us. Don't forget."

He touched Adam on the shoulder. Turning quickly, he ran down the street. When he had gone a little way, he stopped and waved. Wayah waved back.

Slowly Adam made his way back toward the college. It was sad to have to leave such a fine friend as Duncan, perhaps never again to see his redhead or hear his warm laughter. But he would hold fast always his friendship with Duncan. They were brothers forever.

The corn in the college garden was higher than his head, the ears were getting bigger and fuller every day. Soon he would take his leave of Williamsburg. The thought was sweeter than anything the apothecary had to sell.

Back in Chota, what a lot he would have to tell. Who among them would be able to imagine all the riches and great inventions of the whites? Two Sticks and other chieftains who had visited here at times perhaps, but even they had never done and seen and learned all that he had. In his heart he felt very proud and cheerful for having spent this long time at Williamsburg.

A man passed him and stumbled on the rough roadway. "Shove me, you nasty little heathen," he snarled and struck out at the boy.

Wayah ducked and ran. There were things in Williamsburg he would be glad to leave behind, glad with all his soul. He approached the college and ran inside the grounds. Down the path under the trees toward Brafferton he sped.

Suddenly he stopped. There was Mrs. Dawson standing in the evergreen garden. Something was wrong, he could sense it by the stiff and frightened way she stood, the rigid set of her head. He went quietly closer along the row of shrubs.

Three braves in breechclouts stood before her. Tall, strong men with the afternoon's sun gleaming along their bare backs, men who were hunters and warriors and important members of their tribe.

One of them was Two Sticks!

cinatin
den av
Once a
was all

Alon
him, w
as the
had ne

Once
and ge
Wayah
Oh, ho
boy to
home?

Ofte
head o
someti
never a
to be w

But
of it. H
deal th
ther ha
the old
ware.

Since
Her le
doubte
had do
scossit
agreem
things
say tha
duce th

Once
throug

- 14 -

Chota

WAYAH knelt on the creek bank among the autumn-colored leaves of the sumac. With his bow strung and his arrow notched and ready he was tracking a deer. The buck had entered the water and for a minute Wayah thought it must have crossed. But no, something caught his eyes a little further up the bank. There he found the tracks leading back into the woods.

He followed them until he heard a noise. He checked the breeze, shifted a little to the right and crept forward silently once again. Through the bushes he spied the buck, a young one with a fine light-colored pelt. It was rubbing its antlers against a sapling, scraping away the covering of dead skin.

Wayah pulled the bowstring back slowly, slowly, and aimed just behind the foreleg. The deer suddenly tossed its head and trotted off between the trees. Wayah followed as quickly as he could, putting his feet down gently in just the right places so that he walked without a sound.

It was well he had been so quiet for he came up on the buck unbringing this about, even if his part had been only very small. If it had caused him to cease a little to be a Cherokee boy, it was only a tiny bit.

Someone was walking ahead of him on the trail toward the village. It was Fox Who Runs. "Si-yu," the other boy called, turning around. "I heard your feet. I knew you carried game, I could smell it. You hunt a lot, Wayah. You must have a great pile of deer skins."

"Only three," admitted Wayah. "But before the cold weather comes, I hope to have more. I plan to trade them for a white man's gun." He wanted such a gun with all his heart. It was so much easier and better and finer than a bow and arrow.

Fox Who Runs considered this. "I, too, would like a gun," he said. "I would like it very much. But I am not much good with a bow and arrow. My father goes back into the mountains to trap beaver to trade and I'll go with him and get enough pelts of my own to trade for a gun. Perhaps."

"Beaver are scarce these days," Wayah said. "I wish you luck." He shifted the weight of the meat to his other shoulder, as they passed in among the scattered houses of Chota.

"Come home with me," Fox Who Runs said. "Yesterday my mother made a great many corn cakes with huckleberries. My little brother has been eating them all day. I'm afraid he'll be sick unless I eat the rest of them and save him from a pain in his belly."

He grabbed Wayah's arm and pulled. "Come help me save my little brother from this terrible pain."

Suddenly there was a loud outcry. The two boys turned. "It's that new trader from Virginia with his whining voice," Fox Who Runs said. "My father thinks he is bad."

Out through the doorway of the trading house strode Swift River, the brother of Wayah's mother. In his hand was a brand new hatchet. Behind him came the trader shouting and grabbing at the hatchet.

Swift River saw his nephew and stopped. "Wayah, come here and tell this white man that I am not a fool," he called angrily. "And that I will not be cheated."

"My young brother's pain is nothing that requires your great wisdom," Fox Who Runs laughed. "But those two need you, Wayah. How great you are to be able to speak English and settle quarrels among the traders. As for me, I am stupid and ignorant. I can only swim and play ball—and eat many, many corn cakes."

Wayah swung the bundle of meat at him.

"If you find time later, come anyway," Fox Who Runs called over his shoulder. "Your presence would honor us." With a peal of laughter he was gone.

Swift River yelled at him again and Wayah went running. "Yes, uncle," he said.

"I have left three deer skins inside for this hatchet," Swift River began angrily. "He says he will have four. Tell him that it is the same hatchet as the one I have bought in Virginia from white traders for three. He is cheating me. I will have the hatchet for three deer skins or I will sink it in his head."

The trader was babbling away at Wayah. "Tell this here crazy Injun that the going price for that ax is four hides," he shrieked. "He'd do well to give me another hide or the hatchet."

Wayah stared sullenly at the two men. Behind them at the corner of the trader's house he caught a glimpse of Otonee watching, waiting for him to do some foolish thing he had learned from the white men. Oh, Otonee was right and Fox Who Runs was right. It was better to be ignorant and have no other troubles than a bellyache from too many corn cakes.

He said nothing. "Well, Wayah, speak!" cried Swift River. "Tell this stupid white face that I am Swift River and I know a thing or two and that I will have his scalp if he doesn't behave."

"Ain't you the boy did interpreting for me the other day?" asked the trader.

"I do not understand," Wayah said sulkily in Cherokee.

"What do you mean?" Swift River inquired.

"This white man's words are strange," answered Wayah, turning away. "I do not know why he quarrels with you. I do not think I know any English."

Swift River scowled at his nephew. Suddenly the trader jumped forward and tried to take the ax away from the warrior. The two men struggled back and forth. Wayah trembled. He knew Swift River's hot temper. He might easily kill the white man.

"Stop!" he cried, and then in English, "Stop, trader."

The men turned surprised faces toward him. "I thought you done quit speaking Christian language," said the white man.

"I have remembered," answered Wayah. And to Swift River, "Give him the hatchet and I will tell him what you say."

Swift River reluctantly let go of the ax. The two men stepped away from each other, glowering.

"Injun say," Wayah said slowly and warily, "Injun say he get hatchet for three skins. In Virginia. Why you want four skins? Same ax, same skins. Why you want four?"

The trader looked startled. "Ask him does he want to walk to Virginia? Ask him don't he think it's worth a deer skin for my trouble coming all the way down here and now I got to go back? Ain't he ever heard tell things is always a heap less dear in Virginia? I got to get some little extra for the risk in bringing things here to his doorstep."

Wayah considered carefully. "The trader says," he told Swift River, "that things cost more because he has to bring them here. It is a long and dangerous journey from Virginia here. For making this journey to bring you the ax he asks an extra deerskin."

Swift River was puzzled. "I do not understand. I pay for an ax, not for a journey. Three skins is the price of an ax."

Wayah pondered. "Uncle, will you go to Virginia to buy your ax?"

"Go to Virginia!" exclaimed Swift River. "The Green Corn Festival starts soon. After that I must repair my dugout before the weather gets cold. And perhaps go on the warpath against the French. And do much hunting. No, I will not go to Virginia."

"Then you must pay this man for making the journey for you," explained Wayah. "One hide for the journey, three hides for the hatchet."

Swift River thought a moment. "Very well," he answered shortly, "I never heard of paying a man for walking, but if that is the white man's way, I suppose I will have to."

Wayah turned to the trader. "Swift River now understands," he said. "He give four hides for ax."

The trader grinned with relief. "Well, I'm glad it's clear," he nodded. "I ain't trying to cheat anybody. Four hides is the going price."

Wayah picked up the meat. "You're a fine lad," the trader added suddenly.

The boy shrugged. "Sometime Injun ear too small, can't hear what white man speak." He walked off and around the corner of the trader's house came face to face with Otonee. The old man took him by the arm. Wayah was surprised. He had expected his grandfather to turn his back on him.

"You are grown, my son," Otonee said. "Soon you will be a tall man. I have watched you. You are strong and swift and a good hunter. I suspect you will soon be able to take a warrior's place in town affairs."

"I hope so, Grandfather," replied Wayah.

They walked along together. For a minute, even though they did not speak, it was like old times, before he had gone to Williamsburg, and it made him wish he had not left home.

Wayah turned to his grandfather. "You were right," he cried. "Grandfather, you were right about the white man. He cannot touch the red man without hurting him. In Williamsburg I saw how some are made useless and no good by envy and some by hate and even I have split a little, though I have tried not to . . ."

He paused suddenly. He *had* tried, he had tried to see what was good that the white man had, what could help the Cherokees and he had tried not to let himself be touched by the rest, the foolishness.

Yet, in truth, who could split? Who could cease to be an Indian?

Gideon Green Peach was a worthless Indian, but he was an Indian all the same. Though William Squirrel had wanted so badly to be a white man, he had not wanted the white boys to think evil of Indians and had falsely confessed to stealing so that they would not.

Wayah was one of the Real People and would always be. He

"And I'll think of you," Duncan promised. "Come back to Williamsburg some day, Adam, and come and see us. Don't forget."

He touched Adam on the shoulder. Turning quickly, he ran down the street. When he had gone a little way, he stopped and waved. Wayah waved back.

Slowly Adam made his way back toward the college. It was sad to have to leave such a fine friend as Duncan, perhaps never again to see his redhead or hear his warm laughter. But he would hold fast always his friendship with Duncan. They were brothers forever.

The corn in the college garden was higher than his head, the ears were getting bigger and fuller every day. Soon he would take his leave of Williamsburg. The thought was sweeter than anything the apothecary had to sell.

Back in Chota, what a lot he would have to tell. Who among them would be able to imagine all the riches and great inventions of the whites? Two Sticks and other chieftains who had visited here at times perhaps, but even they had never done and seen and learned all that he had. In his heart he felt very proud and cheerful for having spent this long time at Williamsburg.

A man passed him and stumbled on the rough roadway. "Shove me, you nasty little heathen," he snarled and struck out at the boy.

Wayah ducked and ran. There were things in Williamsburg he would be glad to leave behind, glad with all his soul. He approached the college and ran inside the grounds. Down the path under the trees toward Brafferton he sped.

Suddenly he stopped. There was Mrs. Dawson standing in the evergreen garden. Something was wrong, he could sense it by the stiff and frightened way she stood, the rigid set of her head. He went quietly closer along the row of shrubs.

Three braves in breechclouts stood before her. Tall, strong men with the afternoon's sun gleaming along their bare backs, men who were hunters and warriors and important members of their tribe.

One of them was Two Sticks!

- 14 -

Chota

WAYAH knelt on the creek bank among the autumn-colored leaves of the sumac. With his bow strung and his arrow notched and ready he was tracking a deer. The buck had entered the water and for a minute Wayah thought it must have crossed. But no, something caught his eyes a little further up the bank. There he found the tracks leading back into the woods.

He followed them until he heard a noise. He checked the breeze, shifted a little to the right and crept forward silently once again. Through the bushes he spied the buck, a young one with a fine light-colored pelt. It was rubbing its antlers against a sapling, scraping away the covering of dead skin.

Wayah pulled the bowstring back slowly, slowly, and aimed just behind the foreleg. The deer suddenly tossed its head and trotted off between the trees. Wayah followed as quickly as he could, putting his feet down gently in just the right places so that he walked without a sound.

It was well he had been so quiet for he came up on the buck unexpectedly. Once more he pulled back the arrow but this time he let it go. There was a little "thwack!" The deer started off toward the creek.

Wayah followed. There lay the buck at the edge of a canebrake. The arrow had gone almost through it.

Wayah knelt by the dead animal and took out his steel knife and skinned it. When he was done, he sang the ritual song and covered the deer's blood and remains with leaves. It would please Otonee to know that he had done this. It would not please Master Dawson, though.

As for Wayah himself, it neither pleased nor displeased him. Since the day it had dawned on him that his red stone was not a sacred amulet at all, that only his own strength had sustained him at Brafferton, he had begun to have doubts that Fire and Water really cared whether he prayed to them or did the things the Elders said these ancient gods wanted done.

He gathered up part of the meat in the skin and walked back toward Chota. The maples had begun to color, sumacs and black gums were scarlet. One thing was so sure, Wayah thought, that everyone must believe it. There was a great spirit who spun the year through the seasons, winter and summer. Who made all things, trees and birds and Indians and deer, giving them each their proper place in the world.

The Indians knew that proper place. The great spirit had taught the red man better than the white, so that he knew just what things in the forest were good to eat and which were useful for clothes or shelter or medicine. He could live in peace with the world and not try to cut it down or burn it up or fence it in or split it in two.

No matter how many days he spent in Williamsburg, Wayah thought, nor how many books he read, he would never have learned to track a deer so soundlessly nor how to catch fish with bruised walnut bark. Certainly in the town he would not have learned how to find his way through the forest. The Cherokees knew many good things that white men would likely never learn.

He could yet remember the streets of Williamsburg and the thrilling sight of coaches and gaily dressed people and the fascinating shops and the many things that were sold in them. Hidden away safely he had the watch that Duncan had given him. Once a day he wound it with its tiny key, happy to know that this was all the meat and drink the little creature needed.

Along with it he had the Testament Master Dawson had given him, with "Adam Wolf" written in the front in a fine hand, as well as the blue shirt which the Governor had given him but which he had never worn.

Once in a while he thought of Master Dawson, of his kindness and gentleness, and the way he had begged and begged for Wayah to send Two Sticks away and stay with him another year. Oh, how could Master Dawson know what it had cost a Cherokee boy to spend that year at Brafferton or how much he longed for home? Yet, it had been hard to refuse the teacher.

Often, too, he remembered Duncan. He would see that red head or that freckled face among the leaves when hunting, or sometimes in his campfire. At such times he thought he would never again have a friend so gay and so warm-hearted and so easy to be with. So he had split a tiny bit, it could not be helped.

But he was still Wayah, one of the Real People. He was certain of it. He wished Otonee could believe it. It bothered him a great deal that Otonee seemed no longer to care for him. His grandfather hardly ever spoke to him now, though Wayah often found the old man watching him when he thought Wayah was unaware.

Since his return last summer things were going well for Chota. Her leadership over all the towns of the Nation was no longer doubted. Perhaps Chota's Head Man and the Council of Elders had done the most to bring this about as well as to push Ammonscossittee out of power. Who knew what secret meetings and agreements had taken place while he was away at school? Such things were always a part of Cherokee life. Yet who was there to say that Wayah's presence in Williamsburg had not helped to produce this triumph?

Once again there was peaceful trade with the white man throughout the Nation. Wayah was glad to have been a part of bringing this about, even if his part had been only very small. If it had caused him to cease a little to be a Cherokee boy, it was only a tiny bit.

Someone was walking ahead of him on the trail toward the village. It was Fox Who Runs. "Si-yu," the other boy called, turning around. "I heard your feet. I knew you carried game, I could smell it. You hunt a lot, Wayah. You must have a great pile of deer skins."

"Only three," admitted Wayah. "But before the cold weather comes, I hope to have more. I plan to trade them for a white man's gun." He wanted such a gun with all his heart. It was so much easier and better and finer than a bow and arrow.

Fox Who Runs considered this. "I, too, would like a gun," he said. "I would like it very much. But I am not much good with a bow and arrow. My father goes back into the mountains to trap beaver to trade and I'll go with him and get enough pelts of my own to trade for a gun. Perhaps."

"Beaver are scarce these days," Wayah said. "I wish you luck." He shifted the weight of the meat to his other shoulder, as they passed in among the scattered houses of Chota.

"Come home with me," Fox Who Runs said. "Yesterday my mother made a great many corn cakes with huckleberries. My little brother has been eating them all day. I'm afraid he'll be sick unless I eat the rest of them and save him from a pain in his belly."

He grabbed Wayah's arm and pulled. "Come help me save my little brother from this terrible pain."

Suddenly there was a loud outcry. The two boys turned. "It's that new trader from Virginia with his whining voice," Fox Who Runs said. "My father thinks he is bad."

Out through the doorway of the trading house strode Swift River, the brother of Wayah's mother. In his hand was a brand new hatchet. Behind him came the trader shouting and grabbing at the hatchet.

Swift River saw his nephew and stopped. "Wayah, come here and tell this white man that I am not a fool," he called angrily. "And that I will not be cheated."

could not go back and erase the year at Williamsburg from his life any more than William Squirrel could grow a new arm. But surely he had not been made worthless by it, surely there was something to be said for knowing about Williamsburg and white people.

"Grandfather," he began again. "The white men are here. They are numerous as leaves on a tree. They bring many things the Cherokees might use. They have in their lives some few good things. If the Real People are ever going to live at peace with the white men, some of us must learn their ways and how to get along with them."

Otonee nodded. "I know, my son," he said. "I saw Swift River's quarrel. I was afraid. Then you came and I saw it was good that there was a person here who could explain the white people's queer thinking to us. I saw how you made peace and that is good. I have known for a long time that the red man must learn to live with the white man and that can only be done if we learn to understand the whites. You will help us do that. You *must* help us."

He smiled at Wayah. "Not long ago walking in the woods, I saw a thing I had never seen before. A young tree had been struck by lightning and split from crown to root, but it had not withered and rotted. Instead the two halves had healed and each was growing upward toward the sky. There were not two worthless trees, but two strong ones. You are such a tree, my son, for though the lightning has touched you it has not slain you. You have had the vigor to heal yourself and become a tree for the red people and a tree for the white. We will both need your strength in days to come, and I will be proud of you."

Was he two trees?

No, that was foolishness. He was not two trees or even one tree, but one Indian boy. Nevertheless a thing had happened to him that did not happen to all Indian boys. He had a knowledge of the white man and his customs and his language. With that knowledge could he not help his people? Could he not save them some heartbreak in the days to come?

Suddenly he felt he could.

"Thank you, Grandfather," he said. Then he smiled. "I shall be a help to my people. First I will, however, help Fox Who Runs. Take my deerskin to my mother and I will go to Fox Who Runs' house. He has a most terrible need of me. Someone *must* help him eat a great many corn cakes!"

Laughing, he ran off.